LUKE

M. MALONE

gives him what he wants. *Her*.

All I Want: The only thing Kay wants is for Elliott Alexander to stop treating her like she's invisible. But a car accident forces her to reach out to the only man she trusts to save her.

All I Need is You : When the man she loves leaves town after their steamy kiss, Kaylee Wilhelm is done. But when she's targeted by a stalker, Eli is the only one who can protect her.

Just One Thing : Scientist Bennett Alexander is a bona fide genius but he still needs a dating tutor to "get the girl". What could go wrong? Other than falling for his teacher, of course!

The Simmons

Make Him Mine : Trent sees Mara Simmons as the little sister he never had. But she finally has a plan to get him exactly where he should be. *In her bed*.

Make Me Feel : Matt Simmons is over Army doctors until he sees his physical therapist is h-o-t. But Penny wants nothing to do with military men and Sgt. Sexy won't change her mind.

Make Her Stay : Mara has always known Trent is *The One*. But then she discovers the man she loves just might be a stranger.

Bad Business (The Kingsleys)

Bad King: My parents just put a gold diggers target on my back. But if all they want is a wedding, I can do that. I'll find the fiancee of their nightmares. *Who Wants to Marry a Billionaire? Must be completely inappropriate.*

Bad Blood : I'd do anything for my best friend's little sister. Until she asks for the one thing I can't give. One night. No rules. ***RITA® Award Winner!***

Blue-Collar Billionaires

Billions from the deadbeat dad they never knew sounds pretty sweet. Until they find out what he really wants.

Tank / Finn / Gabe / Zack / Luke

- Romantic Suspense -

Shameless / Force / Deep / Sin / Brazen

- Paranormal Romance -

Nathan's Heart / The Brotherhood of Bandits

Contents

LUKE

Chapter One

Luke

I was five years old when I first learned that most people are liars. Ashley Graham told me I was her best friend and kissed me on the cheek. I've never again experienced a euphoric high quite like when she grabbed my hand and pulled me beneath the jungle gym.

I've also never experienced devastation as acutely as the moment I realized she really just wanted me to share the gummy bears in my pocket.

My eyes go back to the email I just received from an old high school "friend" who looked me up on Facebook last month. Brandon was never someone I knew well but at least he wasn't one of the jocks who made my life hell. I hadn't thought anything of accepting the friend request.

It was kind of flattering to have some of the same people who never noticed me before suddenly want to hang out. Until after exchanging a few emails and finding out that he was mainly interested in getting me to invest in his new business. A video series.

Reluctantly I click on the attached file and almost snort up the last of my soda when it opens. It's a promotional poster with scantily clad women mud wrestling in the jungle for a video called Girls Gone Ape.

No, seriously. *Girls Gone Ape.*

After wiping up the drops of soda on my keyboard, I quickly close the file before anyone sees me looking at it. Maybe it's a good idea to wait a little while before I respond to Brandon. Although I'm not sure time will help much. There's only so many ways to say, *hell no, please lose my number.* Luckily, I've been expecting this. Word has apparently gotten around that I've inherited a lot of money and this is the result. People are only friends as long as they want something. Not that I didn't already know that.

Maybe I should look up Ashley Graham while I'm at it and thank her for the life lesson.

I glance through the rest of my emails and then hit the refresh button. All these emails from people I couldn't care any less about and nothing from the one person I truly consider a friend. Now that I have this sudden influx of cash, I wanted to do something to help others so I asked my online buddy C7pher to help me run a coding school for underprivileged kids. We could set it up any way we wanted, hold classes in different parts of the country even. I specifically threw that part in there because I know he doesn't like to be tied to one place for long.

He's suddenly stopped responding to me.

No texts.

No emails.

Nothing.

C7pher has always been secretive. I've never even heard the dude's voice before. But he's gotten me out of more than one scrape online and covered my ass for me before I was skilled enough to do it myself. Now it's like he's fallen off the grid completely.

With a sigh, I shut the lid on my laptop just as my mom rounds the corner carrying a slice of pie and a Coke that I know is for me. She sets the glass down on my table and then continues on. I watch as she sets the pie in front of a man reading a newspaper two booths behind me. He smiles up at her gratefully and even though I can't hear what he's saying, it doesn't take much imagination to guess. My mom is a magician with pastry and all of her longtime customers at her bakery, *Anita's Place*, adore her almost as much as I do. Now that she's started serving a few lunch and dinner options, things are busier than ever.

A few minutes later, she slides into the booth across from me. "What are you still doing here, sweet pea? You're usually gone by now."

Even though her voice is steady, her face shows her relief at being off her feet. She pushes her long braids over her shoulder. She's worn her hair that way as long as I can remember.

"Finn and Tank are meeting me here. They invited me out to have drinks." As expected, that news brings a smile to her face. She reaches a hand across the table and pats my arm.

"That's wonderful, baby. I'm so glad you're getting to know your brothers. Maybe they can convince you to get out there and make some friends your own age. It's not right for you to be holed up here with me and the rest of these old folks."

"Mom, I have friends."

She rolls her eyes affectionately. "You know what I mean. Real friends. Real people that you can see face to face."

This is an old argument so I don't bother explaining again that my online friends are as real as it gets. Unlike the jack-asses coming out of the woodwork to be "friends" now that I have money, my online friends have been there since I was a twelve-year-old hanging out on chat boards because I was lonely. Our connection is based on nothing more than a meeting of the minds and not because they want something.

She sees the look on my face and squeezes my arm. "I just want to see you getting out more instead of staring at a screen all day. You're doing important work online and you know how proud I am of you. But I want you to have other things in your life, too. You know, friends. *Girlfriends*."

"Mom, stop." The blush I feel coming on mortifies me almost as much as this conversation. Somehow, no matter how old I get, my mom can make me feel like a kid.

She holds up her hands. "I didn't say anything."

My phone dings and I pull it out of my pocket to check it. It's a message from my brother, Tank.

"It looks like the guys are going to be late."

Mom stands and then waves to the waitress who just walked in. "I'll just go change now that Rory is here to take over the floor." She kisses me, a gentle buss against my forehead, and then disappears behind the counter.

I'm about to send a message back to Tank when an alert shows up. There's only one person on my email list that I have an alert for. I open my email and then stare in disbelief at the one word answer from the guy I thought was my best friend.

No.

That's it. No explanation, just no.

Another text message pops up from Tank telling me they're on the way. It covers the email I was looking at but it's like it's burned into my brain. More than a decade of friendship distilled down to one word. I don't want to be angry but I suspect the anger is better than what lies just beneath. Hurt.

I quickly type a text back to my brother. "Rain check on tonight. Something came up."

———

That email stays on my mind over the next few days. I've sent several messages to C7pher but he hasn't replied to any of them. Did I do something to piss him off? Or maybe he's worried about the money aspect? Does he think that because I'm funding the school that he'll be obligated to put up the same amount? Maybe I wasn't clear in my original proposal.

Whether I'm working or hanging out at the bakery, the *whys* and *hows* of it are all I can think about. Then it hits me how insane it is that one word from someone can mess with my mind this much.

Maybe my mom is right. Having this level of attachment to someone without knowing who they really are is unhealthy. But knowing that doesn't change the reality of the loss. For years C7pher has been the person I confided in, commiserated with and relied on for advice. My mom tries, she really does, but it's hard for her to talk about my work when she doesn't really understand what I do. C7pher filled a gap in my life that I hadn't even realized was there until he was gone.

We don't even know each other's real names. He only knows me as DarkAngel, the persona I created as a kid. But he's taught me so much and without ever asking for anything in return. If it had just been a No to working on the school with me, I could have accepted it. But as days have passed and there's been no further response from him, I've come to accept what that No really means.

It's a no to our friendship.

C7pher has dropped out of my life as surely as if he never existed. And as much as it kills my ego to admit it, he's one of the few hackers I've met who's better than I am. If he doesn't want to be found, there's nothing I can do about it.

Several days later, I'm working on building the framework for a new suite of security software I'm developing when someone slides into the booth across from me. I look up into my oldest brother's stark face.

For so many years, I was the outsider in my family. The product of my mom's failed marriage to a man who didn't care enough to stick around long enough to meet me. My mom's family is pretty old school. So finding out that my mom had a shotgun wedding to some random white guy during a time when interracial marriage just wasn't done was a shock. My grandpop didn't speak to her for a long time and I know that hurt her a lot. I can't help but feel that I was a constant reminder of her mistake. The pale child that didn't fit in with the rest of the clan.

When I met Tank, it was a shock to realize that I look kind of like him. Well, I look like him minus the scary badass part.

"What are you doing here?"

Tank shrugs and then picks up the menu card pushed to the end of the table and studies it. "Emma's freaking out because the guy she hired to create our wedding website screwed it up and it's not working. She was hoping that you might be able to fix it."

"Sure. Although I have to warn you that I have no talent with websites. The ones I build are functional but not exactly fancy."

"That's better than one that redirects to a porn site."

I choke back a laugh. "Yikes. Are you sure the site is broken or is the guy just pissed off?"

He makes a face. "I may have threatened him. He was a little too friendly with Emma."

"Ah, now I see. It's probably best if I just build you a new one. But you could have just emailed me for that."

Suddenly he won't meet my eyes and is super interested in the menu card he's been pushing around. "I was in the neighborhood."

As many times as he's been here, I'm sure he's got the menu memorized by now and Tank lives nowhere near here. I look over my shoulder and notice my mom watching us. When she sees me looking, she gets really busy wiping down the counter.

"My mom called you, didn't she?"

"Yeah. Pretty much. Plus, I wasn't going to turn down free pie."

"Who said something about pie?" Finn appears at the edge of the table and sits next to Tank, stretching his bad leg out. He props his cane against the wall of the booth. Finn's hair is lighter and he doesn't have a nose that looks like it's been broken multiple times but you can definitely tell they're brothers.

"You guys act like crack addicts with the food here. You might as well just insert an IV and mainline it."

Tank chuckles. "If that was an option, I think Finn would take it."

Finn makes a face. "Hey, I regret nothing."

It's become something of a tradition to give my brothers a hard time when they come and check on me. I spent months trying to avoid them, wanting nothing to do with my absentee father or his other sons but they just wouldn't leave me alone. Now I'm forced to admit that I'm glad they didn't give up on me. After a lifetime of feeling like an outsider in my own family, it's kind of nice to have that connection. Not that I would ever tell them that.

Tank's dark eyes swing back to me. "So, what the hell is wrong with you?"

"Nothing is wrong with me. My mom just worries."

"Is it a girl?"

I miss a key typing and insert a line of nonsense into the code I'm working on. "*Fuck*. No, it's not a girl."

Finn starts playing with the sugar packets on the table. "It's cool if it's a guy. You could tell us."

I snort out a laugh. "Sorry to disappoint you but there's nothing interesting going on. There's no scandalous love drama to entertain you." I falter, unsure of how much more to say. It's difficult to explain the dynamics of online relationships to most people. They just don't get it.

"It's just that someone I thought was a friend ... turned out not to be. I'll be fine."

Finn nods. "We just wanted to check on you. But we'll leave if you'd rather be alone."

I can see in his face that he means it. They'll leave me to wallow in my funky mood if I ask them to. Brotherly concern is still an unfamiliar experience but one I'm starting to find I need more and more.

I look out the window, a little uncomfortable at the sudden serious turn of the conversation. My eyes are drawn to a spot across the street. A girl is standing in the middle of the sidewalk staring right at me. She's completely still, nothing moving on her except for her hair as it blows gently in the wind. People move around her, almost as if she's a part of the landscape.

She's wearing all black and the dark wave of her hair against her pale skin is extremely striking. My heart speeds up and I lean forward trying to see better. There are people around her yet she seems completely, heartbreakingly alone. Like a lost angel. There's also something familiar about her, like a word that's on the tip of my tongue. I feel it through every cell of my being. *I know this girl.*

But I've never seen her before, I'm sure of it.

Finn raps on the table and I turn toward the sound of the noise. He and Tank are both watching me expectantly.

"Luke? You okay?"

Frantically, I turn back to the window. She's gone. My eyes scan the street outside and the sidewalk across the street. It's still raining and the few pedestrians outside are covered in rain ponchos and huddled under umbrellas. But there's no one in all black.

No angels with haunted eyes.

"Yeah, I'm fine." But my eyes go back to that spot on the sidewalk.

I'm not sure why I felt such a sense of foreboding when I saw that girl but it took me off guard. *If I even saw a girl.* I rub my eyes. The project I've been working on this past month has kept me up late. I'm more than likely just seeing things. I shake it off. She's probably a character in one of the RPG games I play sometimes. Because how many people just stand in the rain without moving like that?

Tank and Finn are still watching me. When I finally turn back to the table, Tank narrows his eyes. I can tell that my half-hearted assurance hasn't convinced him.

"Seriously, I'm cool. My mom thinks I must be depressed or something just because I'm not out partying with other people my age. You guys can stick around. It's not like it's the first time I've been disappointed in my life."

Tank pantomimes holding up a tiny violin and playing it.

Even though half of my mind is still on the girl I saw in the rain, I can't help but laugh. "You're such an asshole."

Finn chuckles too and the sound lifts my mood. My mom comes over and sets down two pieces of pie and before he can move, I grab his fork and stab the second piece. His expression of mute horror is so good I wish I'd been recording it.

"Just for that, find your own damn pie."

Chapter Two

Seven

oday I'm going to do it.

I look around the hotel where I've spent the last two nights. There are several shirts thrown over the bed from when I changed clothes three times this morning. My laptop is on the desk and my e-reader is on the nightstand. Normally I'm in and out of hotels so quickly that I barely have time to unpack. But not this time. This time I'm settling in like I'm here on vacation.

Because I haven't worked up the nerve to do what I came for.

Frustrated, I flop down on the bed and pick up the manila envelope I left there this morning. For the first time in three years I'm taking a vacation and this envelope holds the reason why. With trembling fingers, I pull out the contents. My secret shame. A photo of an adorable cherub-cheeked boy.

Lucas Marshall.

For so long the computers at the school library were my only escape from overcrowded foster homes and the pain of being separated from my little sister, Grace. Then I met Luke on a message board. Our friendship over the years became one of the constants that kept me going whenever I lost hope. People at my school weren't exactly lining up to be friends with the weird girl with the scar on her face.

But then I'd log on and Luke would be there with another story about his mom or his crazy uncles. Through his words I disappeared into an existence where there was warmth and happiness.

There haven't been many constants in my life but Luke has always been one of the only things I've been able to count on.

It never occurred to me then what a breach of trust it was to investigate my online friend. In my mind, I was just doing what any teenage girl does when she has a crush. Look for information. Plus, I was young and stupid, eager to put my newfound skills to use.

My fingers run over the rough surface of the photo. It's slightly crumpled and the quality is grainy but considering I had to hack several administrators at West Haven High to get access to their yearbook proofs to get it, it's in pretty good shape.

"Luke" was listed under Extracurricular Activities as editor of the school newspaper so I assumed that was what he preferred to be called. He also appeared really young despite being listed as a sophomore. He told me later that he was thirteen at the time.

Luke had told me himself that his mom had a bakery and a simple search had allowed me to figure out where it was. The website for the bakery *Anita's Place* lists Anita Marshall as the proprietor. I knew he was the only child of a single mom and had a hard time making friends, too.

With every detail gathered, a picture emerged of a boy much like me. He didn't exactly fit into his world, either. We learned together and challenged each other and when he got himself in trouble hacking something he shouldn't have, I was there to bail him out. That day we made a pact to always be there for each other. To be the person the other could call if they needed help. Any time. Any place. He'd promised to always be my friend.

But that was because he doesn't actually know who I am.

His email asking me to help him build coding schools for kids excited me in ways I haven't felt in years. Underprivileged kids often lag behind in technology education simply because they don't have easy access to computers. I spent as much time as possible at the library instead of whatever foster home I was assigned to but even that wasn't enough sometimes.

I was so excited about the project until the ugly truth hit me. To do this, I'd have to meet Luke face to face. He'd finally know what I've taken so much trouble to hide. And everything would change between us.

"Sometimes you have to take a risk," I whisper.

It's been years in the making but it's finally time to reveal myself to Luke. I can only hope he'll understand why I lied to him.

Decision made, I gather up the clothes strewn across the bed. Packing my suitcase will give me something to do while I gather my nerve. Today is the day and no matter what, after this I won't be staying in this hotel. If I chicken out again, then I'll be on the first thing smoking back to New York. Or if I go through with it and Luke is pissed. Maybe he won't want to talk to me. Maybe he won't forgive me.

But if he does ...

If he does then maybe I'll finally have what I've dreamed of for years, the chance to be with him for real.

———

Rain drips from one of my eyebrows and onto my cheek. The awning for Anita's Place is sagging slightly under the rain but it's still easy to read the letters. This is it. There's a good chance Luke is in that building right now.

Cursing, I step under the awning for a business across the street. I clearly didn't think this plan out properly since I have no idea where to go from here. Just because this is where Luke usually hangs out doesn't mean he's in there right now. He could be at a friend's house or even out of town. My heart sinks and I suck in a sharp breath. Suddenly my heart is pounding and I feel like I'm going to be sick.

What if I've come all this way and he's not even here?

Movement in the window across the street draws my eyes. A man sits down in one of the booths. It looks like he's talking to someone. The way the light hits the glass makes it hard to see so I move down the sidewalk a little. That's when I see who he's talking to. Only from the side but the sight still takes me off guard.

The man is on a laptop typing furiously and even though he's obviously much older, *and much bigger*, I think as my eyes roam over his tall frame, it's definitely Luke.

"Hello friend," I whisper.

Looks have never played a part in our friendship for obvious reasons. But I can't deny how unsettling it is to see how handsome Luke has grown to be. My hand goes to cover my cheek unconsciously before I pull it back down. That won't matter to him. I know it won't.

We have a bond that transcends anything physical. I've never been able to get attached to anyone before besides Grace. I have friends, sure. The barista at my favorite coffee shop. I'm friendly with the girl who lives at the other end of the hall in my apartment building and have accepted several invitations to hang with her friends.

I've tried to build connections outside of the virtual world but every single one of them pales in comparison to the way I feel about Luke.

He is the closest thing I've ever had to a best friend.

I'm so arrested by my first sight of him in the flesh that it takes me a moment to notice that another man has joined them in the booth. The two guys sitting across from Luke must be friends since it looks like they're having a pretty in-depth conversation.

This wasn't part of my plan. Stupid as it sounds, it hadn't occurred to me that Luke might not be alone. The first day I was too chicken to even leave my hotel room and yesterday, I got as far as this street before turning around and walking back to my hotel.

Now I finally get the nerve to speak to him and he's not alone? Maybe it's a sign.

"No more running. No more running."

I repeat it to myself until I feel calmer. No matter how hard this is, it's time to reveal myself. He might be angry but all I can do is hope he'll understand.

When I look up, Luke is staring right at me. Caught in his gaze, I can't look away. For those seconds, minutes, hours, time stands still. Then one of the men in the booth leans forward and Luke looks away. The spell broken, I blink away the rain dripping into my eyes.

What the hell was that?

I glance around, suddenly aware that I've been standing in the rain in the middle of the sidewalk while people walk around me. I walk around the corner out of sight. My heart is pounding from just that intense moment.

"Oh, excuse me!" I jump back as I almost slam into two men wearing dark suits. There's a black SUV at the curb. I step back to give them room to pass but they don't move. The hair on the back of my neck stands up as one of them moves behind me.

"Miss Parker?"

Now my heart is in my throat. This last year I've been so careful but what if some of the less than legal things I've done in the past have finally caught up with me?

Not now when I'm so close.

Another man climbs out of the SUV. He stops in front of me and removes his dark sunglasses. He should look ridiculous wearing them in the rain but I have a feeling this is a man who wears a suit and sunglasses everywhere, including the shower.

"I'm Agent Walker." He shows me a badge but puts it away before I really have a chance to examine it closely. "We need to talk."

"About what?" I glance at the two guys with him. Like most repeated lawbreakers, I know my rights. I have the right to ask what they want with me and I also have the right not to answer any of their questions. Keeping your mouth shut is the best defense against any charge.

"Let's take a ride." He gestures toward the SUV at the curb.

I'm already shaking my head. "A ride where? If we're going to a police station then I need to call my lawyer." Too bad I don't actually have one but he doesn't know that.

"I don't think you want to do that."

"Oh is that right? Why wouldn't I want to do that?" His smug attitude is already annoying me.

His eyes gleam. "Because I can help you get something you want. And I think you can help me, too."

Chapter Three

Luke

By the time Tank comes back two days later, I've worked up a pretty decent looking website. I wasn't being modest when I told him that web design isn't my thing. I can create the back end but I have no eye for what looks good. Luckily, Tank forwarded my list of questions to Emma and she gave me some direction.

Emma couldn't come so it's just Tank and I sitting in my usual booth in comfortable silence. Our silence is only broken when my mom brings another Coke for me. She's been trying to wean me off for years but it's my only true addiction. Considering the things other kids my age are usually into, I think she's finally accepted that sugar overload isn't the worst vice to have.

"Did you want anything else, Tank?"

He laughs and rubs his stomach. "No, I think I'd better stop while I'm ahead. I've already had to up my workouts after coming here so much."

Mom balances the plate in the crook of her arm and collects my empty glass. "Life is too short not to eat good food." Then she pats him on the shoulder and moves on to check on the customers in the booth behind us.

"I guess I'll get out of your hair now," Tank says as he stands. "Thanks for doing this."

"Let's just hope Emma likes what I did." I stand too and stretch my arms overhead, stiff from so many hours sitting in one spot.

"She'll love it. Especially since you did it for us. She's sentimental that way. For some crazy reason she thinks you're cute."

Laughing, I shove him toward the door. "Go home. And next time just call. I'm sure you've got more important things to do than come down here just because my mom is worried."

"More important than making sure my little brother is okay? This whole thing has been pretty fucked up but if you know nothing else about me Luke, know that there's nothing I classify as more important than family. And that's what you are."

He claps me on the shoulder awkwardly and it feels like a battering ram drilling me into the floor. Brotherly bonding isn't a thing I'm used to since I grew up as an only child but I'm learning.

"Thanks, man. I really—" I lose my train of thought when a large black SUV pulls up directly in front of the bakery. Two large guys get out of the back and enter. The one in front scans the room and when his eyes land on me, his gaze hardens.

Oh shit.

My mind races, immediately reviewing my activities over the past month or so. Ever since a few brushes with the law as a teenager, I've been careful to keep my nose clean online and stay away from any database or server connected with the U.S. Government. There's no way anything I've been working on lately would warrant a visit from scary men in black suits. Yet, here they are.

"Luke Marshall?"

I nod slowly, noting that the other big guy is standing directly in front of the door, blocking us in. "Yeah, that's me."

"We need you to come with us."

"Wait a minute. Is he under arrest?" Tank takes charge immediately, shifting his large body in front of mine.

My mom comes from the back and then halts when she sees us standing in the middle of the floor. Her eyes roam over the guys in their black suits and then she looks out the window at the black SUV at the curb.

"Luke? What is going on?"

Her face falls and I know what she's thinking. That I've gotten myself in trouble, hacking into something that I shouldn't have.

It kills me I ever caused her so much worry but it hurts a little that she immediately assumes the worst. I haven't been in trouble for years.

"Mom, I swear I didn't do anything."

I've consulted with the FBI before for one of the cyber security task forces but I was always informed beforehand. It wasn't like this.

One of the guys holds out his badge so we can inspect it. FBI. Just as I thought. When Tank is done looking at it, he puts it back in his suit jacket. "We just need to ask him some questions."

By the tone of his voice, it's pretty clear that resisting won't end well for anyone.

I turn to Tank and my mom. "It's no problem. I've consulted with the FBI before. It must be pretty important for them to come fetch me like this. I'll be back as soon as I can."

Tank doesn't look satisfied but puts an arm around my mom's shoulders. "I'll just hang out here and annoy Anita until you get back."

Mom looks up at him gratefully and for the first time, I truly appreciate the brothers that have bowled their way into my life.

"Thanks."

I follow behind the big guy as he leads me out of the bakery and to the SUV at the curb. He doesn't speak, just shuts the door behind me and then climbs into the front.

Even though they haven't said I'm in trouble or anything, something about this feels completely off. Not just the way they showed up out of the blue but the cloak and dagger way they're behaving. There's something they aren't telling me.

"So, any chance we can stop for burgers on the way? I'm starving."

Big Guy and Even Bigger Guy glance at each other in the front seat but don't respond. The atmosphere in the car goes from awkward to hostile and I get the feeling that my participation in this meeting isn't as voluntary as I was hoping.

"Or we could just ride in silence. That's cool, too."

I sit back and watch the streets pass by, hoping I'm ready for whatever the hell I'm neck deep in now.

———

Big Guy One and Two leave me in a sterile white room and file out without another word. I'm getting more and more uncomfortable with the direction of this unscheduled meeting.

Scratch that, I'm pissed as hell.

Previously, my meetings with Agent Walker took place in Washington D.C. I would drive up, get a hotel for the night and spend the next day in meetings with the cyber security division. I was able to provide some insight into certain cases since I had the unique experience of actually pulling off some of the crimes they were investigating.

Allegedly, anyway.

But this is different. We drove for about thirty minutes to Langley Air Force base which is located in Hampton, the next city over from West Haven. We parked in an underground garage and then they led me to this room, no explanation for why I'm here and no indication of when I'll be leaving.

This is feeling less like a consultation and more like a detainment.

The door opens and Agent Walker enters. Luckily, he's by himself.

"Hey, Luke. Sorry about the way you were brought in. I didn't know about that until it was in process."

The apology cools my anger. Slightly. "What's going on?"

He indicates I should have a seat and after a moment of hesitation, I pull back one of the metal folding chairs at the table. I could stand on principle but there's no reason for me to be uncomfortable.

He takes a seat across from me and leans in. "Your name came up in conjunction with another case. If I'd been aware, I would have stopped it before it got this far."

"Wait, you mean my name came up as a *suspect* in another case?"

He winces, so slightly I almost miss it. "You aren't a suspect. We know you're in the clear. You've been a great asset to us over the years."

I lean back, mimicking his casual *we're all friends* posture.

"And of course, it doesn't hurt that you've had me under surveillance for years, either. So you know I haven't been involved in anything illegal."

He goes still. Clearly he thought I was unaware of that.

The agents weren't hard to spot and even after they stopped following me physically, I knew they were watching me online. I was aware of it every time they tried to hack me and sometimes I even let them do it.

Of course, I only let them intercept what I *wanted* them to see.

"Well, anyway. That's not why you're here. We need your help." He coughs and raps his knuckles against the table. "With a suspect."

Okay, now things are getting interesting.

In all the years I've been consulting with him, he's never allowed me to have direct contact with a suspect before. Maybe because I was underage some of that time. Or maybe because he didn't trust me yet. After all, the only reason our paths ever crossed was because I was hacking into the Pentagon.

Allegedly.

Truthfully, keeping me away from the suspects was probably a good call because when I was younger and a little more reckless, I might not have been able to resist the urge to learn.

The guys they're after are usually on a different level. These aren't your run of the mill hackers trying to break passwords so they can steal credit card information or some bullshit like that.

These are guys that want to hack into official databases, topple corrupt regimes and reveal secrets to the world. These are guys with a mission. The top of the food chain.

Guys like C7pher.

Even though I know it's wrong, it's impossible not to respect their skills and their passion. For someone like me, it's a slippery slope.

"There was a breach reported earlier today at Langley. Someone accessed the servers reserved for a special project. A project very few know about. We logged the I.P. address of the unauthorized access and agents were dispatched to the location. It was a warehouse with only one person inside. It's almost like she wanted to be caught."

"*She?*"

He stands and I stand, too. "Yes. There was nothing in that warehouse except for a girl on a laptop."

"Huh. Why would someone hack a government database from an empty warehouse?"

"That's what we need you to help us find out."

I'm following him from the room when it hits me. "You know I'm happy to help out but just out of curiosity, how did my name get involved in this? I mean, why did your boys think I was involved to start with?"

He stares at me for a long while.

"Because when she was first detained, the suspect listed you as her emergency contact. She says she'll only talk to you."

Chapter Four

Luke

$\mathscr{I}$f I thought I was going to meet this mysterious woman right then and there, it was because I'd forgotten the snail speed at which everything government moves.

First, I was presented with a bunch of paperwork to sign, basically agreeing not to ever reveal anything that happened. I've already signed this stuff before but I guess they have a different layer of legalese if you're in actual contact with a cyber terrorist.

It's about an hour later when I'm led down another hallway. There wasn't much time for me to review the folder of information on the suspect. I got nothing more than a name.

Sarah Parker.

It means nothing to me.

Agent Walker stops right outside a nondescript gray door.

"We'll be right on the other side of the glass. Don't accuse her of anything but try to get her talking about her mission. Find out what the hell she was looking for and how she even knew where to start."

"Right. Get her talking. I can do that."

He hesitates and then opens the door. I step inside and wait until I hear the gentle click of the door shutting behind me. The knowledge that I'm being watched behind the large mirror on the wall doesn't help my anxiety any.

The table in the center of the room is empty. I turn around, looking behind me. I'm about to bang on the mirror and ask what the hell is going on when I notice her in the corner.

She's small, so small I almost mistake her for a child. A curtain of long, dark hair covers her so completely that all I can see are the tips of her Chucks. They're electric blue.

Then she looks up.

We stay suspended like that for what I hope is just a few seconds before I find enough brain cells to speak.

It's the girl from the rain.

"Hey. What are you doing on the floor?"

Large, dark eyes continue to watch me as I take a seat at the table. I'm trying not to move too quickly or do anything to spook her. She already looks pale. She's probably terrified.

I remember what it was like being interrogated by agents as a teenager. I fear any sudden movements will just freak her out more.

Aware that we're being watched, I'm unsure of how to proceed. Walker said she put my name as her emergency contact. But I'm positive that I've never seen this girl before that day in the rain.

So why would she claim to know me?

More importantly, what could she hope to gain by using my name?

Not too many people know about my consulting with the department in the first place. There's no way she could have known that my name would even work in her favor.

None of this makes any sense.

The FBI is tiptoeing around this innocent-looking little girl when she looks more likely to hack into the Disney servers to get some free Princess shit.

"Hey, why don't you tell me what happened. I'm sure you didn't do anything wrong."

She'd gone back to staring at the tips of her shoes but at my words, her eyes swing to mine. I almost shift backward in my seat at the sudden cunning gleam in her eyes. This is not some innocent little kid.

"Are you sure about that? I'm no angel."

It's the first time she speaks and the soft whisper of her voice sends a little shiver down my spine. Then she leans forward and once our eyes meet again, she smiles.

"Well, I'm an angel online but only after *dark*."

My heart stops in my chest and as we stare at each other, our eyes play out a hundred conversations that we can't speak aloud. There's no mistaking the emphasis she put on the word dark.

Except for a few slip-ups when I was a teenager, I've been careful about covering my activities online and there's only one person who has been around long enough and is skilled enough to figure out my real identity.

If she knows about my online alter ego, DarkAngel, then there's only one person she could be.

C7pher.

As soon as the thought occurs, it's disregarded as impossible. Maybe she just happened to choose a strange way of phrasing things.

As if she can sense the shift in my thinking she says, "You always said if I needed you, just call."

In those few moments, my entire world realigns and everything I thought was real becomes a dream. After all, how can you rely on anything if the person you've trusted the most isn't who you thought they were?

I stand so fast the metal chair screeches against the floor. Just before I reach the door, she calls out.

"Luke!"

My hand stills on the doorknob. There's nothing we can say with an entire roomful of agents watching. The conversation that needs to take place between us cannot happen here.

Because no matter how pissed I am, I can never forget that this is the one person who can destroy me.

"Just a minute, *Sarah*. I need to explain to Agent Walker that there's been a misunderstanding."

I deliberately raise my voice and turn toward the mirrored wall. A few minutes later, Agent Walker comes in.

"What's going on, Luke?"

I point at Sarah. "I didn't realize who you had in here. She's not a terrorist. She's a white hat. Top Fortune 500 companies hire her to test their systems. She tries to break in the same way any other hacker would, then provides them with an assessment of their vulnerabilities."

Walker glances between the two of us suspiciously. "So, you do know her? Why didn't you say so?"

"I, uh, didn't recognize the name at first."

Sarah stands then and glances at me. "Luke and I have fallen out of touch recently."

"You were on a job when they grabbed you, right?"

She nods. "But it's all supposed to be confidential so I wasn't sure if it was safe to talk. But yeah, I was hired by a private company to test their security. I had no idea that was a government server until it was too late."

Agent Walker doesn't look completely satisfied but at least he doesn't look quite as hostile.

"Sarah is skilled enough that if she was trying to hack into something unauthorized, she wouldn't have done it without rerouting through some foreign ISP first."

Agent Walker nods as if he has any idea what that means.

"I'm sure Sarah can show you the emails from the company that hired her. That should give the FBI something to go on in tracking these guys down."

"Of course," Sarah agrees quickly.

"And we can go back to my place and catch up."

They both stare at me.

"W-What? Your place?" Sarah swallows and then glances over at Agent Walker. "Right. I am pretty tired."

"Now, wait a minute—"

I hold up a hand. "You would have had me under surveillance when I left anyway. Now you can watch us both together. Look, you know she's not behind this. It was obviously a setup and she's going to cooperate fully. At least let us get some sleep."

I can tell he doesn't like having the decision taken out of his hands but doesn't have a good reason to stop us. And I have no doubt that the look in my eyes is pretty scary right now.

Because I have a mission of my own tonight.

To interrogate the beautiful little liar who has been trolling me for the past decade.

———

The ride back home is even more awkward than the ride in. A different set of big scary guys drives us back to the bakery. Even though they drive off, I have no illusions about privacy. They'll be nearby watching our every move.

Through the glass, I can see my mom talking to a customer. She and Tank are going to want an explanation and I have no idea what to tell them. Despite how adamant I was about this plan, I'm wondering if it's really a great idea to bring this chick I obviously know nothing about back to my place.

But then I remember who she is and more importantly what she knows. If she'd wanted to hurt me, she could have done it by now a million times over.

"I never thanked you for cleaning up behind me."

At the puzzled look on her face I add, "The Pentagon."

Then, for the first time, she smiles.

"That was a hot mess. You were smart enough to proxy through a few servers before you attempted to hit their network but not smart enough to delete the logs. It's a good thing you bragged about what you did otherwise I wouldn't have had time to get them all!"

As hard as it is to believe this hauntingly beautiful girl is C7pher, with just a few sentences I know without a doubt it's true.

"Why did you? I always wanted to ask why you would have put yourself at risk for a kid too cocky to realize how much he didn't know yet."

She turns and looks over her shoulder at the bakery behind us, the carefully detached expression she's been wearing melting into obvious longing.

"It was the way you talked about your mom. It was obvious how much you loved her. Through your stories, I got a glimpse of the one thing I've never had. A family. And your family became mine. Truthfully, I think you saved me long before I saved you."

I wish I could hold on to the anger. Anger would be so much easier than this. Her words touch me in a way I wasn't expecting, moving me to sympathy and then to shame.

All the things I take for granted are things she's never had.

"Thank you for covering for me back there." She digs her hands in her pockets.

The motion makes it even more obvious how thin she is. Too thin.

"You're welcome, Sarah."

She chuckles. "It's Seven. No one calls me Sarah unless I owe them taxes."

Seven. Somehow as soon as she says it, it makes sense. Her name fits her.

She runs her hands up and down her arms as if warding off a chill.

"I guess I should get going then. You should get inside. I'm sure your mom is worried."

I've complained about my mom's overprotective nature so many times over the years. But now every complaint seems so petty and ungrateful. All those times I complained to her and she has no one. How shallow I must have seemed.

"Come inside. Let's get something to eat. The goon squad dragged me away before I got any dinner."

She hesitates. "You don't have to do that. I know you were just saying that to get out of there."

My stomach chooses that moment to rumble loudly.

"I was bluffing my ass off for sure but not about that. Come on. Besides, I meant what I said about us talking."

She looks cornered, like an animal in a trap that isn't sure whether to show its neck or snap your hand off if you get too close. But I need to know her deal. If she walks away from here tonight, she'll disappear, FBI surveillance be damned.

"I think I deserve more than a one word email, don't you?"

Her eyes meet mine and then she nods slowly.

"Yeah, you do. But you might not like what you hear."

Chapter Five

Seven

When I imagined meeting Luke for the first time, I dreamed up every possible scenario. My favorite was that fate would somehow throw us together and Luke would fall for me without any idea who I was.

I also imagined that I would one day be confident and cool enough to just walk into the bakery where he spends so much time, sit down across from him and introduce myself.

I never imagined it would be in a cold, sterile room while we were being watched by the FBI. And I *never* thought I would have to lie to him.

Maybe he isn't the only one who has gotten cocky over the years.

As I follow him into the bakery, I dimly register the old-fashioned decor and the waitresses in their crisp white aprons. The air smells like sugar and spices and every wonderful thing and just being there is like being wrapped in a warm hug.

Luke stops to talk to someone and I hang back, not wanting to intrude but the truth is I want to throw myself right in the middle of it all. I want to belong someplace like this, where everyone knows each other and there's enough love to go around.

Luke motions for me to come closer. As I step up beside him, the man he's talking to glances at me. I instinctively shrink back.

Geez, he's huge. Luke is tall but this guy is even taller and built like a mountain.

"Seven, this is my brother Tank."

I glance at Luke uncertainly before extending my hand. But as soon as he looks at me, the big guy breaks into a smile that looks like it might crack his face.

"Nice to meet you. I wasn't sure any girl would put up with this guy." He glances at Luke with a strange expression and I catch Luke rolling his eyes.

"Oh, we're not—" I gasp in a slight breath when Luke squeezes me to his side so hard I lose my train of thought.

"Seven hasn't eaten yet, so I'll see you later. Thanks for staying with Mom while I was gone."

"Of course. I'll call you later."

Luke leads me to a booth in the center of the room. He still has a tight grip on my waist and warmth travels through me at the unexpected touch. He gestures for me to sit in the booth and then to my surprise, slides in next to me.

"Something's about to happen and I need for you to play along. How's your poker face?"

"My poker face? It's pretty damn good but we're not playing poker."

A woman stops next to the table and puts a glass of soda down in front of Luke. Her long dark braids are held back by a ribbon that matches the blue of her uniform. Then she looks from Luke to me and back again and smiles brightly.

Luke heaves a little sigh next to me.

"Hey, Mom. Sorry about earlier."

My attention snaps back to her in surprise. Now that I'm looking, I can see a slight family resemblance, though her skin tone is much deeper than his. With her wide smile and bright eyes, I would have never guessed she could be old enough to be his mother.

"Mom?" I squeak.

Luke glances at me. "Seven, this is my mother, Anita. Mom, this is Seven. My girlfriend."

My eyes widen slightly before I remember his comment about maintaining a poker face.

"Hello! It's so nice to meet you. Luke has told me so much about you."

She glances at him with a fond smile. "He has? Well, that's nice to hear."

Luke leans forward. "I didn't have time to eat anything earlier and Seven's hungry, too. We'll take whatever the lunch special was today if there's any left."

Anita clasps her hands together. "Of course! I'll bring you some of the corn chowder and some bread."

She takes one final glance between us and then practically skips off.

He glances over at me. "That wasn't as bad as I expected."

"You told her I'm your girlfriend because..."

"What else was I supposed to say? Hey Mom, this is my best friend that I didn't know was a girl until an hour ago?"

"I see your point."

We sit in silence for a minute before he blurts out. "Were you ever going to email me back?"

My eyes roam around the diner, taking in the people eating their goodies and talking with their companions. How can I make him understand? Someone like Luke has always had a place, always been surrounded by people who love him.

But none of this is usual for me.

The idea of unconditional love and acceptance is about as comfortable as a new shoe.

"I was going to email you back. But I needed time to figure out how to approach you. I wasn't ready to let it go yet."

"Let what go?" he asks.

"You."

We're interrupted then as Anita sets down a glass of water for me, two bowls of steaming soup and a plate of bread. Luke thanks her and she leaves but not without another pleased smile in my direction. It warms me, that smile, and without saying another word it seems that Luke understands.

He lifts his chin toward the bowl. "Eat. We have a lot of work to do later."

Obediently, I take a big spoonful of soup, my toes curling as the creamy broth hits my taste buds.

"Work? I have no work to do. I finished with my last client before I came here."

The last part of the sentence dies in my throat when I remember I'm not supposed to tell him that. I cover with a little cough and reach for my water.

He hands me a piece of bread. "Work is probably the wrong word. We have *stuff* to do. First, we have to figure out this whole thing with the FBI."

"You're going to help me? Even after ... everything?"

"Of course I'm going to help you."

He looks uncomfortable but finally meets my eyes. He doesn't exactly look happy with me but there's something there that melts all the tension and stress of the past twenty-four hours until I'm suddenly very tired.

"Thank you, Luke."

He pushes the bread plate closer and turns back to his bowl, a slight blush coloring his cheeks.

"Don't thank me yet. Just eat. If you're good, you get pie."

———

*A*fter I finished my bowl of soup and more helpings of bread than was probably wise, Anita brought out pieces of pie that were almost as big as the plate. I'm stuffed and replete, the warmth of the pie making me sleepy.

Most of the other customers have left except for a few die-hards in the corner booth and the other waitress has gone home for the night. Anita takes off her apron and hangs it on a hook by the swinging door into the kitchen.

That must be some kind of signal I'm unaware of because Luke tenses. He grabs my hand and then tugs me out of the booth. After retrieving his laptop from behind the counter, he pulls me toward the door.

"Well, we're going to go. Night, Mom!"

Anita waves and I'm sure I must look like a deer in head-lights as I follow Luke out into the soft night air. He's still got a hold of my hand and the warm pressure around my fingers is really distracting. But I don't say anything, just let him lead me across the gravel parking lot to a sporty little black convertible.

"Cute car."

He shrugs. "I figured I should spend my money on some-thing other than computers for once."

I settle into the plush interior and let out a sigh of appreciation. How different would things be if I spent my money on a few more creature comforts? If I could save up a little nest egg and make a place for myself somewhere? No more chasing the craziest job offers, no more risks for the highest payout.

But as sweet as that sounds, the things I'm working for mean more to me than my own comfort. Anything else is just a fantasy.

"So, where are we going?"

Luke fastens his seatbelt and waits until I do the same before he pulls out of the parking lot. I've never been to Virginia before but West Haven reminds me of several of the small towns in New Jersey where I lived as a kid. Lots of trees, cute little houses that look like they hold happy little families.

Places I never belonged.

"My apartment is close by. I usually hang out at the diner just so that my mom isn't alone at night. But now I've hired her private security, which she doesn't know about." He glances at me.

"Hey, I won't tell her."

"So I don't have to stick around as late anymore. My brothers recommended I do that last year and it's taken a lot of stress off my mind."

We take a few more turns and then he pulls up in front of a modern apartment complex. Considering what I know about his situation, it's not as fancy as I was expecting but then maybe Luke is like I am. Saving his money for more important things than impressing others.

I follow him inside and up two flights of stairs. He opens the last door on the hall and ushers me inside. There's a small lamp burning on the side table next to a beige couch. The rest of the apartment is dark.

Luke walks around, turning on lights and then sits down on the couch. Unsure of where to go, I perch on the edge of the cushion next to him. All of my stuff is still back at my hotel.

"You could have used anybody's name for your emergency contact. So, why me? After that email, I was pretty sure you didn't want us to meet."

I close my eyes, fighting exhaustion. When I open them, Luke is watching me. His dark eyes make me feel things. Things I'm not ready to examine just yet. But he deserves an explanation, especially after the way I blew him off.

"When we first met online, all those years ago, it was at a time when I'd just been put into a new foster home.

Remember when I told you that I don't like staying in the same place for too long?"

He nods slowly, his eyes following my every move. I can feel him assessing me, trying to figure me out.

"I remember. I figured you just didn't want to be tied down."

"Being tied down isn't the problem. I've just never had anyone who wanted me to stay. The first family was fine until they took custody of their nephew. Then they couldn't keep us both."

He shakes his head. "Sorry. That sucks."

"I was moved around to a lot of different situations that were temporary for various reasons but as I got older, it was harder and harder to place me. And when things got really bad ..."

My hand goes up to my cheek again and Luke's eyes follow the movement. His jaw clenches. Suddenly, he doesn't look so easygoing anymore.

"Someone hurt you?" he growls.

"One of my foster fathers ... I accidentally knocked over his drink. And well... the bottle was handy, I guess."

His face twists into a mask of outrage. I look away, unnerved by the display of such raw emotion. This is why I don't discuss my past. It's just too hard.

"I don't know why I just told you that. I don't talk about this stuff. Ever. Anyway, after that my grandmother took us in until she died. She had a lot of health problems but she did her best. Those were good years."

"*Seven*." His head falls forward. "I didn't know it was like that."

"No one did. But you helped me through it."

His face betrays his shock. "I didn't do anything. I mean, *fuck*. I wish I'd known how bad it was and maybe I could have helped. I don't know how but I would have done *something*."

He runs his hands through his hair, leaving his fists on top of his head. He looks so frustrated. His concern touches me.

"You *did* do something. You were my friend. No matter where they moved me, they couldn't keep me away from a computer forever. You were the one place I could always come back to."

"The one person you could call," he says, echoing what I'd said to him earlier.

His face is so expressive. Every emotion shows in his eyes. He's fighting some sort of internal battle and I know my deception has damaged the trust between us.

But over the years, through all the bad stuff, our connection was the one thing I could count on always being there.

Waiting for him to decide whether to trust me is agony. But when it finally happens, I can see it in his eyes before he even opens his mouth. Even though it's what I want, it's also one of the most painful moments of my life because I know before it's all over I'm just going to hurt him again.

He turns to me, his dark eyes intense.

"So, tell me what happened with this job. *Exactly* what happened."

———

He settles back into the couch to listen, resting one leg over his knee.

I'd really rather not recount the story but I can't deny that I would be curious in his place. Especially since I've always been the savior in our relationship, strange as it is.

"I was contacted through my website to do a security analysis by a new company last week. The guy seemed legit on the phone and filled out my survey no problem."

"What kind of things do you ask on the survey?"

"The usual stuff. What their expectations are and what kind of security protocols they currently have in place. Usually that gives me enough information to devise a plan."

He nods. "After that, they asked you to come here?"

"Not at first. I attempted to access their server immediately, then tried the usual methods to gain access. I sent an email to one of the administrative assistants listed on their website claiming her account had been compromised and she needed to sign in immediately. She took the bait. It only took me ten minutes and I was in."

Luke is nodding along with everything I'm saying. What I'm describing is hardly a sophisticated hack, just your standard phishing expedition. They're so popular because they work the majority of the time unless you claim to be an African prince in possession of a stolen fortune.

If you craft a phishing email well, you can gain access to almost anything.

"How did the warehouse come into it?" He stands suddenly. "Do you want some coffee? Tea? Sorry, I'm not a very good host."

It's funny that he thinks so when I'm more comfortable here than I've ever been anywhere else. Talking to him in person feels just as natural as when we've chatted online. It's so surreal to have a conversation and be able to watch his facial expressions and hear his tone of voice.

"No, I'm fine."

I stand and follow him into the kitchen. After he sets the coffee to brew, I pick back up the story I memorized beforehand. I have to tell it just right or it won't pique his interest.

Curiosity is the downfall of almost all hackers and Luke is no different.

It's what I'm counting on.

"Anyway, I was scheduled to meet with them in the afternoon but I arrived a little early. I had already figured out how to get in to the system earlier but because I connected again from that location, that's how the FBI knew where I was. I'm not surprised they were able to trace me but I wouldn't have thought they could subpoena my IP address from the phone company that fast."

"They have priority so they can move pretty quickly when they need to," Luke comments absently.

"Yeah, I figured that out when they burst through the door. Scared the hell out of me."

He pulls down a mug from one of the cabinets. "It's all going to be okay. You know that, right? Agent Walker is intense but I've worked with him a few times before and he's fair.

Mostly, anyway. They'll find who hired you. But I bet we find them first."

I pretend to think about it for a few minutes.

"Do you think that's a good idea? Will you get in trouble? I'm sure the FBI doesn't like anyone poking around their investigations."

He laughs. "You only get in trouble if you get caught. I once changed the date of one of my meetings with Agent Walker on his calendar because I forgot about it."

"Did he ever figure out you hacked him?"

Luke gives me an incredulous look. "His password was his dog's name. What do you think?"

Despite how serious this is, I can't help laughing along with Luke. I know how tempting it is to do those kinds of things just because you can. Most people have no idea how vulnerable they are to being manipulated by people like us. Everyone is one password away from having their entire lives hijacked but most have no idea.

It's probably better if they don't.

He brings his coffee to the table in the living room and then collapses back down on the couch. I sit next to him, inhaling his scent. Already it feels second nature to be this close to him, feeling his warmth.

"You're tired."

My eyes pop open at his voice and I jerk upright. I hadn't realized I'd slumped over.

"Sorry to fall asleep on you."

"Don't apologize for being a normal person. Anyone, except for weirdos like me, would be tired by now. Especially after everything you've been through today."

He stands and I watch as he disappears into the back. A few minutes later, he reemerges with a towel, washcloth and a T-shirt folded on top. I accept the bundle and trail him to the small bathroom in the hallway.

"I can get your stuff from the hotel while you get ready for bed. Where's your key?"

"You don't have to do that."

It's an instinct borne of selfishness because suddenly I don't want him to leave. I have to soak up all the time with him I can.

Before he hates me.

"It's no problem."

Reluctantly, I pull the key from my pocket. I don't really love the idea of Luke carting all my stuff around but it's nice of him to offer. I'm exhausted and practically falling asleep on my feet.

"Just hang out here and I'll be back. By the way, is there anything else you remember about the guy who called you?"

I hesitate just a beat. "Not really. Oh yeah, he had an accent. Sounded Irish I think."

Luke pauses, and then nods his head. "Irish? Are you sure?"

"Yeah. Definitely."

He taps the doorjamb and then walks back down the hall but I still see the look on his face.

Intrigued.

Mission Accomplished.

Chapter Six

Luke

Retrieving Seven's stuff from the hotel didn't take long since it looked like she'd barely unpacked. I combed the room carefully, making sure that her laptop bag and suitcase were all she'd brought. By the time I got back to my apartment, the light was off in the bathroom and I couldn't hear any movement in the guest room so I left her stuff up front. It's late and she probably needs sleep more than anything in her suitcase. I move quietly down the hall and into my room.

I pull out my cell phone as I drop down on the bed. My thumb moves over the screen until I have my father's number on the screen. After months of ignoring his attempts to make contact, I'm put in the position of calling *him*. I really don't want to do it but I haven't stopped thinking about what Seven said.

Irish. There's no way that's a coincidence.

Before I can think too hard about the consequences, I hit the number. Fuck it. I'll just leave a message and deal with it tomorrow. It's late and I'm not really expecting an answer so I'm startled by the soft, well-modulated voice that answers almost immediately.

"Hi. Sorry, this is Luke Marshall. I need to speak with my father."

"He's already asleep. Would it be okay if he called you back tomorrow? I'll give him your message first thing in the morning."

"Sure. Thanks."

I hang up, surprised at how awkward that was. Talking has never been my strong suit but I'm particularly unprepared in this case. What am I going to say? The only piece of information I have in this case is that the guy sounded Irish, which tells us basically nothing. For all I know, Seven got the accent wrong. It could have been a Welsh accent or something completely different.

I peek out into the hallway. The door to the second bedroom is closed and it's all quiet. She didn't ask for anything so I assume she's okay. The entire time I've lived in this apartment, I've never had guests so I'm sure my hospitality leaves much to be desired.

I close my door and then strip quickly, tossing my sweatshirt onto the end of the bed and stepping out of my jeans. I walk into the hall in just my boxers. Goosebumps spread over my skin as the cool air hits me. I walk quickly because it would be just my luck for Seven to step into the hall at this exact moment and catch me half-dressed. Not that I'm in bad shape. The second bedroom she's sleeping in is my office but also doubles as a gym since I have free weights in there. Since I'm sitting so much, I put extra effort into my workouts to make up for it but I'm still not used to walking around shirtless.

Under the hot spray of water in the shower, I let my head fall forward and enjoy the steam. I soap up and then wash my hair. My hand fumbles the bottle and it hits the floor. I pause but I don't hear anything so hopefully the noise didn't wake her. It's so weird to think that she's right on the other side of the wall.

Weird but also slightly arousing to think that she's so close while I'm naked.

The thought makes me fumble again and I finally just set the bottle on the floor of the shower. Imagining her on the futon wearing my shirt and a smile is way too easy. It screws with my head that she's so beautiful but it doesn't feel right to be thinking about her that way. It's like she's trying to take up two spaces in my head, friend and fantasy, and I can't reconcile the two.

Although maybe that's an accurate description. She's been a friend but mostly in my head. The connection I thought we shared was mainly of my own imagination.

The thought is depressing so I dry off quickly and then wrap the towel around my waist. Back in my room, I climb into bed nude and then shut off the light. But it's a long time before I fall asleep.

———

The next morning I wake before the sun. My first thought is of the beautiful girl sleeping in my guest room. I'm struck with the need to see her, to make sure the prior day wasn't some weird dream.

Excitement spurs my movements and I practically throw the covers aside.

After dressing in jeans and a T-shirt, I cross the hall and pause outside the second bedroom. It's quiet.

"Seven?" I listen for a moment but I don't hear any movement. She's definitely still asleep.

Of course she's still asleep weirdo. Normal people aren't awake this early.

I'm actually glad she's asleep. Otherwise I'd have to explain why I'm standing outside of her door like a stalker. Mentally berating myself for my crazy behavior, I walk to the kitchen to get the coffee started and then pause at the edge of the living room. Seven is curled up in a little ball on the couch. Her face is scrunched up into a little grimace and her long hair is all over the place. She doesn't look comfortable at all. Then her eyes pop open.

She sits up and yawns. "Oh, hi."

I pick up one of the throw pillows from the couch that got tossed on the floor. "Is there something wrong with the futon in the office? If it's not comfortable, we could have switched. I've slept in there before."

"No, it's fine. I just ..." She looks vaguely uncomfortable. "Prefer the couch. I usually work until late and fall asleep on my couch most of the time anyway."

Understanding dawns and I regret my offhand question. She's been on her own a long time and shuffled around a lot. I know she didn't have a lot of money for a while and she once confided that she was living out of her car. Back then, I only knew her as C7pher and since I'd assumed she was a guy, it hadn't seemed as scary.

Maybe it's sexist that it bothers me more to think of a girl being homeless but the idea of her that vulnerable hits me hard. Anything could have happened to her out there.

"I understand that. Back in junior high, my mom and I were sharing this one-bedroom apartment so I used to sleep on the pullout couch in the living room. It was years before I could get used to sleeping in a bed, even after I started making money from my software."

"Yeah it's hard to change what you're used to." Her eyes shift to the coffee pot. When I pull down another coffee mug, she smiles gratefully.

"I brought your luggage and computer from the hotel last night. Send me the emails from the guy who hired you. I'll get to work on tracing them and see what I can find."

The wary look comes back into her eyes. "Luke, you really don't have to. I can do it."

"I know you can. Better than I can. But sometimes it helps to have someone else working on it. Someone who has some objectivity, you know?"

She concedes the point with a small nod and then pours a cup of coffee. "Thanks for the help. Even though I seem ungrateful, I truly do appreciate it."

My attempt to shift the attention away from her works and she seems to relax. After she turns on her computer, she forwards me the emails and then disappears into the back, pulling her suitcase behind her. She emerges five minutes later wearing jeans and a sweatshirt with a picture of the Wi-Fi symbol on it. Her hair is pulled up into a high ponytail and she looks so damn young.

After a quick breakfast and my required cup of coffee, I show Seven my tentative plans for the coding school.

It's surreal to be talking about this to someone who actually understands why it matters so much and she has some really great insights to add. Technology programs in most schools aren't where they should be yet and girls especially aren't encouraged to pursue it.

For the first time, I really see what she means. The same reasons she was scared to out herself to me are the obstacles we need to help these kids overcome. There has to be a significant outreach to girls in order to overcome that stupid stigma that technology is a guy thing.

It's almost lunchtime by the time we're done. When I look over at Seven, her eyes are closed and her head is resting against the back of the couch. She's clearly tired so I stand carefully, trying not to disturb her, and move to the kitchen table.

I decide to use the time to investigate the emails she forwarded to me. The email headers give me enough info to figure out the location of the sender.

Dungarvan, Ireland.

So the guy didn't just sound Irish, he was actually in Ireland when he sent the email.

A sense of foreboding has my hands pausing on the keys. What if Max is somehow part of this? Do I really want to know? I've been staying away from him for a reason but what if there's something I can protect Seven from?

With a little frustrated groan, I get up to make more coffee. This is something I'll have to think on for a while. I want to help but there are some boxes that once opened, you can never close again. Before I do anything I can't take back, I need to be really sure. Hell, maybe the FBI will figure it all out and I won't even have to get involved.

Satisfied with that possibility, I decide to tinker on my software design while Seven is sleeping. This software will be designed to make any home or business run more efficiently. Software like this already exists but my version will take it a step further. Not only will the client be able to turn off lights, control temperature, and set the alarm from the web interface but there's also a component that integrates with their banking system. They'll be able to pay bills, order maintenance checks on appliances and schedule maid service. It'll be like a virtual butler that runs your home for you once you input a few parameters.

Working on something new is always exhilarating and before I realize it, three hours have passed. I glance behind me to where Seven is still asleep. She hasn't stirred once.

I kneel on the floor next to the couch and tap her gently on the arm. After a few moments, she swallows and then rolls toward me. Finally her eyes open. The soft, sleepy look on her face makes my heart roll over in my chest.

"Hungry?"

Her eyes trail down and stop at my chest. Then she smiles. "Yeah."

I swallow hard. It somehow feels like we're talking about more than food. It's an effort to halt the dirty thoughts that start running through my head. Her soft, husky voice makes just that one word sound like foreplay but that doesn't mean she wants me to take it that way.

Down boy.

"We can go into Norfolk or Virginia Beach for lunch, if you want? It takes a little longer to get there but we'll have more choices."

She sits up and stretches her arms overhead, the hem of her sweatshirt rising enough to show off a patch of taut, pale skin on her belly.

"We're not going back to the bakery for lunch?"

"Uh, no."

It's impossible to miss her pout. But she follows me outside to my car and when she says that she's okay with burgers, I drive one city over to New Haven to The Rush. It's an old school diner with great burgers and shakes. I honestly would have eaten cardboard if it meant I didn't have to see anyone I know.

After we order and Seven is working on sucking down a chocolate shake, I finally relax. She looks around and then says, "I like this place. But I still don't understand why we couldn't go to the bakery. I really wanted to see it again."

"We'll go back again, don't worry. Before long you'll be sick of the place. I just can't keep bringing you there. It'll only get my mom's hopes up."

"Isn't that what you wanted?" She looks confused. "Otherwise, why tell her that I'm your girlfriend in the first place?"

"She thinks I'm alone too much. If she thinks I have a girlfriend then maybe she won't stress out so much about me dying old and alone. But I don't want to put you through an Anita Marshall inquisition."

She slurps up the last of her shake. "I think it's nice that you're so close to your mom."

"My mom raised me by herself and her family wasn't that supportive in the beginning. So yeah, for a long time it was the two of us against the world. I adore her. But she can be pretty aggressive when it comes to protecting her baby boy. If you thought that FBI interrogation was bad, they've got nothing on my mom. She was probably mentally measuring you for a wedding dress last night hoping to get you locked down before you come to your senses."

Seven laughs, shaking her head in disbelief. "Oh come on. It can't be that bad. Like you don't have plenty of girlfriends already."

My heart starts beating a little faster. Is she flirting with me? I've never been good at this part. When you spend most of your time communicating with a computer, it's difficult to gauge when someone is being sincere or just being polite. Computers don't require social niceties so I'm aware that I'm a little deficient in that area.

"Not really. I'm always working and I can never think of much to say on dates anyway."

"I get that. The last guy I dated was a waiter who was enrolled in the theatre program at NYU. He was a nice guy but I couldn't exactly tell him about it when I had a bad day. He had no clue what I was talking about ever."

"Right? That's a legitimate thing that my family just doesn't get. Dating someone who has no clue what you do for a living and doesn't share most of your interests doesn't really make much sense anyway."

"What are you saying— we nerds need to stick to our own kind?"

Our eyes meet and I'm suddenly having a hard time swallowing. "Well, I guess so."

"Good to know." She finishes the last bit of her burger, swiping a little bit of ketchup off the plate and sucking it off her finger.

The blast of heat takes me off guard. *What is it about this girl?* She's not even my type. I usually go for tall, curvy and bold. But Seven has the kind of beauty that sneaks up on you. Even the way she tips her head so her hair covers the scar on her cheek is charmingly self-deprecating. She makes me want to shield her from anything that might scare her. Despite the inner strength I know she possesses, everything about her seems delicate from the graceful curve of her neck to the long, slim fingers that I'm now imagining wrapped around my dick.

I cough and have to grab a napkin at the last minute to keep from spitting my food out on the table.

"Yeah, I think I'm done." I can feel her eyes on me as I gather up our trash and carry it to the bin near the door.

Helping Seven was the right thing to do and I would do it again in a heartbeat. But there's no doubt that it'll be for the best when we catch whoever set her up so she can move on. This girl has my hormones going haywire and she's only been here a day.

––––––

My phone rings later that evening. Seven is in the office working on my desk and I'm camped out on the couch. I pick it up absently and then answer quickly when I see that it's Agent Walker. After we hang up, I walk back to the office and rap on the door. Seven looks up.

"Agent Walker just called. You're officially off the hook."

She swivels in my office chair until she's facing me. "Really? That fast?"

"Yeah, the emails led them back to a fringe International terrorist group that they've been tracking for years. They must have gotten frustrated at their inability to gain access and decided to hire someone else to see if they could do it."

"That's awesome."

Strangely, her words don't match her expression. I've been in her position before and there's no relief quite like knowing that you're no longer at risk for jail time. Well, in my case I would have been sent to juvie but that was essentially the same thing in my mind. Yet Seven seems kind of under-whelmed for someone who just got out of a pretty serious situation. I would have expected a little more excitement or at least a smile.

"Agent Walker seemed pretty sure that they would get the guys this time so maybe this will turn out to be a good thing."

Seven puts her hands behind her head and sighs. "It shouldn't have happened. I'm getting soft. Staying in one place too long does that to you. You get too comfortable. Complacent."

Her words make me think. Over the years, I assumed that her moving around wasn't something she enjoyed but it was just the hand she'd been dealt being in the foster care system. But now that she's on her own, she could settle in one place if she wanted.

If she wanted. The question is whether she even wants to stay. Will she leave now that she's not under investigation anymore?

"Is that why you said no? Because it would have tied you down?" I lean back against the door jamb, resting my head on the frame.

She watches me with wary eyes. "You know why I said no."

"I would have been cool with it. You could have just told me."

She gives me a *get real* look. "Being taken seriously is hard enough but when most of the people I deal with online have the maturity of a twelve-year-old boy, it's even harder. That's about how old you were when we met by the way. Do you really think your ego could have handled knowing the person teaching you all that stuff was a girl? Or would you have been scared of catching cooties?"

She's right but it doesn't mean I'm ready to admit it.

"Anything would have been better than blowing me off and leaving me to wonder why."

Her face softens at that.

"Why do you think I came here? I came to make it right. But that was just as stupid as this fantasy of being a part of a family. Because I was right to be scared to tell you. The way you looked at me when you found out. The way you're looking at me *right now*. It'll never be the same, will it?"

Her words give voice to the same fears that have kept me up at night. No matter what else has happened, I don't want to lose the special connection we've always had. It shouldn't matter what she looks like. She's still C7pher.

"It won't be the same, no."

Her face falls. I push away from the door and kneel next to her. When I take her hand, she tries to pull it back but I hang on tight.

"It doesn't have to be the same. It can be better. It can be whatever we make it."

Her hand flexes in mine and then she turns it over until we're palm to palm. It's a shocking intimacy to feel that heat, one I like way more than I expected. When she goes to pull her hand back, I let her even though part of me wants to hang on.

She looks around. "So is that offer to crash still open?"

"You want to stay here?" The shock is evident in my voice and I'm sure the expression on my face completes the picture.

"That was the deal, wasn't it?"

"Well, yeah but …"

I extended the invitation to stay with me while working on the project back when I thought she was a guy. I figured it would make the most sense. When developing software, I tend to work around the clock and I'd assumed it would be the same way while we developed the curriculum for our classes. Staying together would make collaboration easier.

But that was before I knew that I'd be in danger of a constant boner every time she's around.

"But what?" she taunts. "You said it shouldn't matter who I am, that you'd still have made the same offer anyway. So, I'm saying yes. Is the offer still open? Or am I booking a ticket back to New York?" Her left eyebrow ticks up in challenge.

I can tell by the set of her mouth that she's already planning her trip home. She thinks she's calling my bluff and that I won't want to work with her now.

What she doesn't know is the real reason I want to rescind my offer isn't because she's a girl but because she's a *gorgeous* girl and I truly can't see how us working together is going to work.

Besides me walking around with a permanent hard-on.

I'm tempted to just let her think I'm a misogynist instead of a horny bastard but then I remember her face last night looking into the bakery. Seven Parker has known too much disappointment in her life already and I don't want to be one more person who lets her down.

"Yes, the offer to crash is still open. We'll work on the project. It'll be fun. No funny business, I promise. I'll treat you the same way I would have if you'd been a guy."

Surprise and delight shines in her eyes before it's banked behind her usual expression of distrust. "Really?"

"Yeah, but don't get too excited yet. You might change your mind and book that ticket to New York when you see how much work we have to do."

Chapter Seven

Seven

After the challenge I threw down last night, I thought he'd want to get to work right away but Luke insisted we do nothing but chill. He ordered some Chinese which we ate in front of the television. We didn't do anything that I haven't done any other night of the year in my apartment in New York. It was a completely ordinary night.

Other than the fact that I was spending it with Luke.

As many times as we've chatted online, talking face-to-face allows for an entirely new dimension to our conversations. He has such an expressive face and before long I could anticipate his reactions just by the way his eyes narrow or how his mouth quirks to one side when he's amused. It's alarming how quickly I've become attuned to his moods.

And how barren my life will feel once he's no longer in it.

When I wake up, he's gone but there's a blanket draped over me and the television is off. I sit up and glance around, pushing my hair off my face. The thought of Luke tucking me in fills me with guilt.

He's trusting me with his dreams and I'm betraying him.

As I stand, every muscle in my body protests. I might have to abandon my story of preferring the couch at night. My back feels like it might have a permanent curve in it after sleeping all cramped up.

"Good morning."

I jump at the sound of his voice. "Morning. You're up early."

"Need coffee. You want some?"

The sight of Luke in the kitchen fiddling with the coffee maker is so homey that it's hard to watch. Emotion floods through me and for just a moment I allow myself to be a complete and total girl. Like, full-on, giggly, Hallmark card ridiculous. I turn away so he won't catch sight of the way I'm grinning like a fool.

It's just that this scene is so close to what I've imagined. Things I'm too embarrassed to admit I long for. Having a cute boyfriend who makes me coffee. To wake every day to that goofy smile and the tender look in his eyes that says he's glad to see me.

That isn't the only thing that says he's glad to see you.

I glance over at Luke again and my eyes drop to the loose-fitting pajama pants that ride low on his hips. Pants that aren't as loose-fitting as they should be in the front.

I can feel my cheeks burning as I spin around. My movements are jerky as I kneel and collect the blanket, folding it carefully and placing it on the back of the couch.

"Yeah, I want some." The double meaning of the words hits me as soon as I say them and I shake my head. "I need coffee in the morning, too. That's what I mean."

Luke watches me as I walk around the room, feigning interest in the books he has stacked on the end table and the pictures on the walls. There's one thing that I haven't seen since I arrived.

His laptop.

I haven't seen anything other than the desktop in his office and after poking around the first night I can tell he doesn't use that much. Considering who *he* is and considering who *I* am, the omission seems deliberate. He doesn't trust me yet. Even though it's going to make things harder for me, my respect for him jumps a few more notches.

"Are you okay?"

"Hmm?" I turn from the window and then accept the mug Luke hands me.

After blowing the surface gently a few times, he takes a tentative sip from his own mug, watching me over the brim.

"Yes, I'm fine. Just looking around. This isn't what I always imagined your place would look like."

"Oh?" He raises his eyebrows but I can tell he isn't mad. His eyes crinkle a little at the corners and I get the impression he's laughing at me behind his cup.

"No. I was expecting more of a bachelor pad. With black leather everywhere and tons of video screens."

He laughs. "Sorry to disappoint you with my boring taste."

"Not boring. Normal. Refreshingly normal."

"That's probably the first time I've ever been called normal."

Our eyes meet in a moment of complete and total understanding. Neither of us has ever been the type to fit in. Being outside the norm, a weirdo, a geek, whatever word people want to apply to us is a part of what drew us to each other.

But when we're together like this, I don't feel strange or different.

"So, I couldn't sleep last night and I was thinking. I need to make some changes."

He deposits his coffee cup on a side table and then pulls out a folder. When he hands it to me, I open it to see the same list he sent me over email. His proposed curriculum for his coding school.

"Changes to your class list?"

He shrugs. "Everything. I added a few more things to the list but it feels... I don't know. Incomplete."

I scan down the list, reading the new things he's added to the bottom. It's mainly security stuff for the more advanced students like fuzzing, Trojans and how to spot a DDoS attack.

He leans closer, his arm brushing against mine as he drags his finger down the tentative curriculum he's drawn up.

"Some of these are going to be for the later classes, obviously. But I just wanted to get my ideas on paper. Just as a start."

"It's a great start. But ..."

"What? You have an idea?" When I hesitate, his voice deepens. "I really want your input, Sev."

The rumble of his deep voice rolls through me and I shiver inwardly. Usually I hate it when people try to nickname me but when Luke does it, it feels different somehow. Personal.

"Well, when I was first learning to code, it was difficult to practice since I didn't have ready access to a computer."

"Right." He nods encouragingly.

"I would jot lines of code down in my notebook and study them when I got home. So I was thinking maybe we could provide some printable sheets and exercises in addition to the online tests."

As I talk, I can feel myself getting excited. This program would have made such a difference if it had been around when I was a kid. Even if I didn't have a computer, if I'd had someone provide me with pre-printed worksheets that I could study it would have been so much easier.

"That's a great idea. Looks like you're saving my ass all over again, huh? I didn't even think about that." He jots *printed worksheets* at the top of the page in his neat, block handwriting.

"Really?"

"Yeah." He looks at me strangely. "This is exactly why I wanted your input. You'll think of all the stuff I'm missing."

My breath whooshes out in relief. "I just didn't want you to think I was trying to take over your project."

I glance over at Luke. He's watching me with a little smile on his face. It's always tricky to propose new ideas for someone else's projects. This is a pet cause for him and I don't want him to think I'm being critical. But to my surprise, the little grin on his face spreads until he bites his lip and looks down.

"Feel free to take over anything you want." He looks up at me, his dark eyes following the movement of my hand as it tugs on the ends of my hair.

The warmth that's been steadily building as we sit so close together, magnifies. I tuck my hair nervously behind my ear even though I really want to pull it over my face and hide a little bit. God, it's so hard to look at him this close. He smells so good and he has the longest lashes I've seen on a man. When those eyes swing my way all I can think about is all the ways I'd like to take over.

Mainly by climbing on top of him and seeing if his lips are as soft as they look.

"Okay," I whisper. It's all I can think of to say but his eyes glow with approval.

I can feel the old insecurity bubbling up and I want to untuck my hair and pull it forward to cover my scar so badly.

But the way he's watching me lets me know he has no problem with the way I look.

———

Over the next week, Luke and I work on the curriculum for his school. I thought it would be awkward, especially with the latent sexual tension brewing between us. It's been a while since I lived with anyone and it's an experience I wouldn't have thought I would enjoy.

Although I've lived alone for years now and I've never thought I was lonely, this past week with Luke has driven home how solitary I truly am. I eat alone. Sleep alone. And when I need company, I go to my favorite coffee shop to people watch. Then I would chat with Luke over IM in the evenings. Instant messaging probably doesn't sound like a conversation to anyone else but for us, it was everything. He was everything.

But in just a week's time, Luke has managed to make me feel like I'm an important thread in the fabric of his life. Not for a moment have I felt like I'm in his way or cramping his style. We work separately on our own projects until the afternoon, and then we move over to the bakery so he can keep an eye on his mom.

By the third day, I was ready to go before he even told me. I've absorbed into his regular routine without missing a beat.

He seems to really enjoy having someone to bounce ideas off of and collaborate with. And I've found myself seeking out his opinion or advice throughout the day, as well. Sometimes, I think I don't even want the advice but just to be close to him.

He really listens when I talk and the way he watches me ... Damn, it's addictive to be the center of his focus. Even though he looks so intense, like he's imagining every variation of dirty thing he could do to me, there's no doubt in my mind that if I asked him to he could repeat back everything I've said. Luke seems just as turned on by my mind, debating every topic with me from the best RPG games to the perils of a capitalist society.

Our discussions are as stimulating as any physical touch and by the time Friday rolls around, I'm one big throbbing mess of sensation. But he still hasn't touched me. He promised that if I stayed here, we would work together the same way we would have if I had been a guy. Luke is sticking to that promise.

His ethics have never been more inconvenient.

This morning Luke decided that we needed to get out of the house so we're sitting in the park enjoying the first official day of summer. The foliage above us is a brilliant explosion of green and I take a moment to close my eyes and enjoy the breeze. A change of scenery is nice and it's definitely sparking my creativity. I pull up one of my unreleased game designs. Art was always fun as a kid but I just didn't have the skill for it. Luckily designing graphics on the computer is a little easier with the right tools. Especially the way I do it.

"Are you working on one of your games?"

I look over my shoulder at the sound of his voice. He leans closer and squints, trying to see the screen in the bright sunlight.

"Yeah. I'm working on a new version of my bestselling game."

My computer is angled away from him so he can only see part of the screen. Luke has always known that I design games on the side but I never told him which ones. I knew he wouldn't be able to resist poking fun. And I understand why. It *is* pretty ridiculous. But there's no use in trying to hide it anymore. If I'm going to stay here for any length of time, he'll eventually see me working on it and figure it out anyway. After a moment, I sigh and turn my laptop so he can see what I'm working on.

That's when he loses it.

His laughter rolls out of him until he falls to the side, his laptop sliding off his lap and into the grass.

"Shut up! It's not that funny." But I betray myself when a little snicker escapes.

My eyes go back to the vector image of a misshapen pig on my screen. The snout is deliberately big and there's a maniacal light in his eyes. It looks like a homicidal mutant pig.

"It is funny. It's fucking hilarious. I can't believe *Pig Punt* is one of your games. How could you not tell me that?"

He's still laughing but seems to have mainly recovered.

"This is why I didn't tell you. You think I don't know how stupid it is? But this is my highest selling game. It was number one in the app store for over a week!"

Luke leans closer and I freeze, all my righteous indignation gone now that his soft breath is wafting against my neck.

"This is pretty epic. Trust me, I'm in awe of your genius. I only wish I had thought of it first. But I have to ask. Why are the graphics so bad?"

Then he's laughing again, except he muffles the sound against my shoulder. The sensation goes straight between my legs and I have to clench my thighs together before I embarrass myself by moaning out loud.

Does he even realize what he's doing? His mouth is pressed against my neck while he's laughing away. He's turning me on and he doesn't even seem affected.

"People like it," I mumble, trying to get my mind back on the conversation. "The cruder the drawings are, the more popular the games seem to be. How else can you explain why misshapen piglets being punted across the screen is so popular?"

"No idea but it's definitely fun. Hell, I have it on my phone, too."

"Well, I'll send you the demo version of this new one once I'm done. It's called *Pig Punt in Space*."

We both laugh at that.

"The things we do for money."

At my words, Luke's laughter abruptly dies. I could hit myself for bringing it up. He has only told me a little bit about his absentee father but I know money is a sore subject for him.

"Sorry. I could have phrased that better."

He shrugs. "You aren't telling me anything I don't already know."

A few moments go by and since he doesn't seem averse to talking about it, I decide to just ask. "Did you meet him yet? Your father?"

He shakes his head.

"Are you going to?"

His head swivels toward me. "Why are you asking me all these questions?"

Stung by the sharp tone of his voice, I turn back to my laptop. "Never mind. It's none of my business."

At that, Luke blows out a frustrated breath. "It's not that. Of course you can ask me anything. I just don't like talking about him."

His phone rings and the look of relief on his face is almost comical.

"Excuse me for just a second. I have to take this."

He answers and then walks a few feet away, leaving me sitting on the grass alone.

———

While Luke is occupied, I pull out my own cell phone and call Grace's social worker, Amy. Ever since I got the idea of taking custody of Grace, I've worked toward that goal tirelessly. Amy has been a huge help and really seems to have Grace's best interests at heart. My distrust of the system is so ingrained that it was hard for me to believe at first but she's been helping me every step of the way.

She answers on the first ring.

"Hi Amy. I was calling to see if there's any news."

"Not yet, I'm afraid. These things take time. But I really don't want you to get your hopes up. A judge is going to want to see evidence of regular employment to prove that you can handle supporting yourself and Grace."

"But I told you, I have money."

"I know, Sarah. But it's not enough to just have money. The judge wants to see that you have a steady income. The nature of your work is unpredictable and you can never know for sure how much money you'll earn each month. That doesn't look good on paper."

This is exactly what she warned me about last time but it's no less frustrating to hear it again.

"You don't understand how important this is. You've never been in foster care. *I have.* I really need this to go through."

Her voice softens. "I'm sorry I can't give you better news. I just want you to be prepared."

Now I feel guilty. It's not her fault that my petition for custody is likely to fail. If only I'd taken legit jobs earlier then I'd have a few years of documented income. But I didn't realize why that would matter back then. I just thought that if I had more money, then I could help my sister. But it turns out that all the shady jobs I took are just one more mark against me if anyone finds out. Agent Walker's words run through my mind again.

I can help you get something you want. And I think you can help me, too.

My heart clenches at the thought. The means to get everything I want lies in how quickly Luke trusts me. And how effective I am at stabbing him in the back.

My little sister's future depends on whether I'm willing to betray the one person besides Grace that I actually care about.

"Thanks anyway, Amy. Sorry to keep bothering you."

"You're never bothering me, Sarah. I want what's best for you and Grace."

"I know. Thanks."

After we hang up, I glance behind me. Luke is still on the phone, his back to me.

And his laptop is on the blanket next to me.

My heart speeds up. This is exactly what I've been waiting for. Luke guards his laptop carefully and never leaves it behind. But after spending all week with me, his guard is obviously down. He left it open right next to me. I reach into my tote bag and pull out the flash drive.

My eyes dart over to Luke as I lean closer to his computer. All I would have to do is insert this and open the file on it. Two seconds and I could be out of here. All my problems would be over. I could go home secure in the knowledge that my petition for custody of Grace would go through and all of my past indiscretions forgiven. But as my hand hovers over the machine, my fingers shake slightly and the flash drive lands in the grass.

Damn it.

I lean over, running my hands over the soft blades, searching for it. Once my fingers brush over the cool metal, I quickly stuff it back into my bag. Luke is still on the phone facing the other direction so it's unlikely I'll get caught but I tell myself it's too risky. That it makes more sense to wait until I have a clear field. Like when he falls asleep or goes to the bathroom.

All the while I'm ignoring the part of me that knows the truth. I could do it now but I just don't want to. I'm not ready for our time together to be over.

When I look up, Luke has turned so his profile is visible. A second earlier and he would have seen me leaning over his computer. My heart is still beating double time so I close my eyes and take several deep breaths. When I open my eyes again, Luke is walking back.

"Sorry about that. That was my brother, Tank. Apparently he forgot to remind me about their rehearsal dinner. Tonight."

"Oh. Oops."

"Yeah, exactly." Luke's lopsided smile makes me feel even more guilty. "So we have to leave. I'm sorry to rush you."

"It's no problem. You definitely don't want to miss that." I only brought my laptop so he'd bring his so I quickly close the lid and transfer it back into my tote bag.

"Definitely. Especially since I'm in the wedding and actually need to practice. I'm one of his groomsmen. Hey, I'm sure they wouldn't mind if you came to the rehearsal dinner, too."

Luke stows his laptop in his bag and hooks the strap over his shoulder. He glances over at me, a pleading look on his face. "It'll be way less boring if you come with me."

Even though he sounds annoyed by having to go, I think a rehearsal dinner with family and friends sounds nice. It would be so easy to go along, imagining that whole time that I really belong here with Luke and his circle of friends. In his life.

But I know the truth.

I don't belong here. And once Luke discovers the real reason I'm staying with him, he won't want anything to do with me. The longer I hang out with him, the more attached I'll get. It's better if I stay behind tonight and finally accomplish what I'm here for.

"Actually, I'm kind of tired. I think I'll stay behind. Maybe get some work done."

He looks disappointed but as usual, he's understanding about it. Luke gets my weird moods in a way no one else ever has. It's dangerous to spend this much time with him and it's only going to make my mission harder. Because every day I'm with him, I wish that I didn't have to go.

Back at his apartment, I sit on the couch with my laptop while Luke disappears into his room. Ten minutes later, he comes out dressed in a neat pair of khakis and a blue collared shirt with a dark blue blazer.

"Wow. You clean up well."

He laughs softly but I can tell he's pleased by the compliment. "I can't embarrass my brother. He's already in the doghouse since he forgot to remind me. Are you sure you'll be okay here alone?"

"I'll be fine. I'm used to being alone, Luke. It's how I prefer to be."

He nods and then stoops to press a kiss to my forehead. "Okay. I'll be back in a few hours."

Shocked into silence, I watch wordlessly as he leaves. The skin on my forehead is tingling, like the place where his lips touched is extra sensitive now. It takes me a few minutes to get my equilibrium back but once I do, I stand up and walk slowly down the hall to his room.

Ten minutes later, I'm forced to concede defeat. Despite how much fun we've had and that kiss, it's obvious Luke still doesn't trust me. His laptop isn't in his room, the guest room, the bathroom or anywhere else I looked.

It's gone.

Chapter Eight

Luke

As I'm driving to the restaurant where Tank told me to meet him, my mind keeps going back to what I overheard. I'm fully aware that no conversation ever sounds right from the outside but there was no mistaking the desperation in Seven's voice. Whatever she needs "to go through" must be extremely important to her.

Maybe it's related to one of the games she's designed or hell, it could have to do with a bill she paid before she left. There's no end of the ways I could fill in the blank on that conversation. So why can't I let it go?

Maybe because you saw her leaning over your computer?

I barely got a glimpse, more an impression of movement than

an actual image but it was enough to make me wonder. Seven has been acting so strange since she got here and after overhearing her conversation, I'd be a fool not to wonder if she has an agenda.

But what?

I can't think of anything I have that she'd want. She makes her own money so I seriously doubt she finally made contact with me to try and rob me. The look on her face when she thought I saw her messing with my computer is hard to discount though. She looked guilty as hell and there's only one reason she'd look that way.

She's up to something.

I'm still turning over the possibilities when I arrive at Sweetie's, an upscale restaurant in the city of Newport News. There's valet parking but my old habits are hard to break. It wasn't that long ago when I was still counting every dollar I made so wasting it on letting some other person park my car seems pretentious. There's a parking lot on the side of the building and when I turn in, I recognize Finn's beat up old pickup truck. It makes me smile. It's definitely not the kind of thing you'd expect a billionaire to be driving.

After parking a few spaces over from Finn, I get out and jog around to the front of the building. I don't think I'm late but

I definitely don't want to put Tank any further in the dog house with his soon-to-be wife.

As soon as I step inside, I spot Tank standing near the check-in desk while a nervous waiter hovers behind him. He lets out a huge groan when he sees me.

"Good, you're here. Em has been freaking out for the last half hour."

"Sorry it took so long. I wasn't at home when you called." I follow him as he weaves between tables. The room they've reserved for the event has been decorated with red and silver streamers and there's a bunch of white balloons right outside the door.

"If you wouldn't mind pretending that I called you a few days ago to remind you that would be great."

I laugh at Tank's nervous look. "You're scared, aren't you?"

"Yeah, you try living with her. We'll see how brave you are then," he mutters.

"If the offer is open—" I break off at the suddenly murderous expression on his face. "Kidding. Totally kidding."

We both laugh but our amusement is short-lived because Emma appears out of nowhere.

"Luke! You're here!"

I'm pulled down into a hug and then before I know what's happened, I'm being hugged by a succession of boisterous, chatty women. Finn's wife, Rissa, hugs me and then pushes me down the aisle to where everyone else is waiting.

"Go see Sasha and she'll tell you what to do."

I walk to where my brother Gabe and his fiancée, Sasha, are standing. I blush as I always do when I see her. With her long curly hair and brown sugar skin tone she reminds me of a pop star I've had a crush on since I was a kid.

Gabe looks pained as she throws her arms around me. My brothers all seem to have found really affectionate women who enjoy hugging.

And I enjoy how much it annoys them.

"There you are! We're about ready to start." Sasha grabs my hand and leads me to the other side of the room and down a long hallway. Then we're outside. A large arbor has been constructed on the lawn behind the restaurant with several rows of chairs set up before it.

"Okay, wait here while I get the other guys. Then we can start."

Soon I'm joined by Gabe, Finn and Tank. Zack finally comes out a few minutes later. He's grown in the sides of his hair to cover the tattoos on his scalp and tamed his signature dark

Mohawk down with some gel. The girls gather on the other side around an older man in a dark suit that I assume must be the minister. He shakes hands with Tank before continuing down the aisle to the other end.

For the next hour, he leads us through the rehearsal. I'm not sure why we need to rehearse walking up front several times but then I see the stressed look on Emma's face. It's apparently bad luck for the bride to rehearse her own wedding so she's standing off to the side watching everything.

When we're finally done, Tank lets out a long sigh of relief.

"This had better go off without a hitch. Emma didn't want to have it here but all the local churches were booked a year out. We had to get creative. This is the only place that could take us so soon so I convinced her to try it. I didn't want to wait a full year to get married but if something goes wrong, she might never forgive me."

"Of course she'll forgive you."

Tank shakes his head. "She hasn't been too happy with me lately. No matter what I do, it seems like it's wrong."

This isn't the kind of thing I expected to hear the day before they're getting married.

He claps me on the shoulder and seems to shake off his prior mood. "How are things going with you? Are you bringing your girlfriend to the wedding?"

"Can I? I didn't want to assume anything."

"You're family. This is a celebration of family so please bring her along. And Luke, if you care about this girl, don't let her get away."

"I don't know how I feel about her."

This is the wrong time to unload on him when he's dealing with so much but I don't know who else to ask. Out of all of my brothers, he's been in a stable relationship the longest.

"How are you supposed to know that you can trust someone that much? How did you know Emma was right for you?"

A faraway look comes over his face. "Because seeing her was what made me look forward to getting up in the morning. If you find someone you can't wait to see every day, that's how you know."

———

When I enter my apartment a few hours later, Seven is curled up on the couch hugging a throw pillow to her chest watching television.

"Luke, you're home!" Her eyes light up when she sees me.

When was the last time someone cared enough to wait up for me? I honestly can't think of anyone else who's ever cared that much besides my mother. I'm just as happy to see her. All I could think about tonight was how much longer until I could come back home and tell her about it.

If you find someone you can't wait to see every day, that's how you know.

Tank's advice comes to mind immediately. But then I remember that she's keeping something from me. Until I figure out what it is, I can't take anything she does at face value.

I close the door behind me and put the take out boxes of food that I brought back for her on the coffee table.

"You had leftovers?" She sits up, adjusting the throw pillow behind her back as she does. With her dark hair in disarray around her face, she looks adorably rumpled. She's also not covering her face. I've noticed when she's tired or caught off guard, she forgets to be self-conscious about it.

"No, that's for you."

Shock then pleasure filters across her face. "You didn't have to do that. That's so nice."

Her smile warms me through and through. She always seems so surprised by kindness.

"How was the rehearsal dinner? Was your whole family there?"

I grab her a fork from the kitchen and she smiles gratefully before digging in to the macaroni and cheese I brought.

"You remember I told you about not knowing my father?"

She nods while taking another huge mouthful of macaroni. It's hard to stifle my laugh. She looks so happy with it, like a little kid being allowed to have junk food for the first time.

"Well, my father had other children before he met my mom. Of course, I didn't know that until recently. Tank, Finn, Gabe and Zack are my half-brothers. We've been getting to know each other over the past year and surprisingly, I like not being an only child."

Her eyes follow mine as we both sit back deeper into the couch. The noise from the television recedes into the background and it's just the two of us cocooned into a little space of our own making.

"Is he having a bachelor party?" Seven asks.

Just hearing the words *bachelor party* makes me groan.

She looks over at me in amusement. "Oh boy, now I know there's a story behind that."

"Hell yeah, there is. Tank's bachelor party was two weeks ago. His bride insisted they have the bachelor and bachelorette party weeks in advance so they wouldn't look hungover in the pictures or in case anything went wrong. It turns out that was a really good idea."

Her eyebrows lift. "Why, did you guys all get really drunk?"

I kick my feet up on the coffee table to get more comfortable. "I didn't but my brothers did. We went to one of the strip clubs in Virginia Beach and they got a table in VIP."

"Pretty swank."

"Exactly. Sounds like it should be a good time, right? I don't even like clubs and I was enjoying myself. Well, everyone was having fun *except* for Tank."

Seven crinkles her nose. "Why not? It was all for him, right?"

"It was supposed to be but he dragged his feet through the whole thing. First he didn't want a bachelor party at all. Then he finally agreed to let Finn plan one but claimed he didn't want strippers. Of course, Finn insisted. Tank was pissed at him until he found out that Emma was having strippers at *her* party."

Seven snorts so hard she almost chokes on a bite of her food. I'm laughing too just recounting the whole mess.

"Did he crash her party or something?" she asks once she catches her breath. "*Please* tell me he crashed her party and fought some male stripper for her honor."

That mental image sets us both off laughing again.

"No, although if he could have found out where it was I don't doubt that he would have. Finn finally calmed him down and he was behaving but when we got to the club what does Tank do? He proceeds to get shitfaced and spends the entire night telling the strippers trying to give him lap dances all about Emma and how much he misses her."

"Aw, now I feel bad for laughing. That's really sweet. All he wants is her."

"Yeah those two are the real deal. I have to admit Tank is pretty funny drunk and *very* chatty. It was a bitch of a time getting him out of there at the end. My brothers each took a limb and then just dragged him out."

Seven giggles at that and I turn toward her. When she sees me looking, she covers her mouth with her hand. I reach out and tug it down. Her laughter trails off and she dips her head so her hair covers her face slightly.

"What?"

"Nothing. I just don't want you to cover that sound. I love hearing it."

"Hearing what? Me laughing?"

"Yeah. I like hearing you laugh. Seeing your smile."

My words hang in the air between us. Seven doesn't seem to know how to respond but I can tell by the flush in her cheeks that she likes this, too. With a little embarrassed laugh, she turns her attention back to the carton of food in her hand.

After finishing the last of the macaroni, she lets out a happy, satisfied sigh and rests her head on the back cushion of the couch.

"I love talking to you like this," she blurts then looks morti-fied at the outburst.

"You do?" I turn toward her.

"It feels just like when we used to chat every night. You always had some crazy story to tell about your family or your newest projects."

"I was always worried you'd get sick of listening to me bitch."

She shakes her head. "You weren't bitching. Just sharing your life. It made me feel like I was a part of it, too."

Taking a chance, I grab her hand which is resting on the couch cushion between us. Although she freezes in place at the contact, after a moment she squeezes my hand.

"That's because you are a part of it. A really important part. And I loved sharing those stories with you. It meant a lot, having someone willing to listen."

In the time that we've been talking, I've moved a little closer. Close enough that when she turns her head to look at me, her hair brushes against my cheek. It's so soft and I wonder how it would feel against my skin.

"There's something else I'd love to share with you if you're willing."

At my words, she looks up. When she realizes how close we are, she swallows. Hard. All it would take is for one of us to lean forward a little and our lips would touch. It's so tempting but until I know I can trust her, it would be foolish to allow myself to get any more attached. It's crazy how this girl has me so turned around.

My gut tells me she's hiding something but it also tells me that she cares for me. So which do I believe? The only thing I can think of is to keep her close and hope that she'll confide in me the way she has before. In order to do that, she needs to know I'm here for her as a friend.

As difficult as it is to rein my lust in, our friendship has to take precedence over my sudden curiosity to know what she tastes like.

"Would you be my date for the wedding?"

Her hand jerks in mine. "You want me to come with you? Really?"

Giving up my resolve to give her space, I pull her against my chest. She's tense for a second and then she melts against me. Her head settles in the curve of my shoulder and her breath warms my neck. I run my hand up and down her back soothingly.

"Yes, I want you to come with me."

"Why?"

Her soft question throws me. Does she really not know how much I enjoy spending time with her? I thought it was pretty obvious that I've gotten way too attached to having her around over the past week. But maybe it's time I make it a little more obvious.

"Because there's no one else I'd rather share it with."

Chapter Nine

Luke

The next morning, I drive Seven to the small strip mall on the other side of town since we don't have time to go across the water to one of the big malls in Norfolk or Virginia Beach. I was going to just call up Sasha and ask to borrow a dress but when I made the suggestion Seven told me I was "such a guy."

I have no idea what that means but apparently borrowing a dress is the worst idea ever.

Following a girl around while she tries on clothes is pretty much my idea of a waking nightmare but luckily Seven seems to know what she wants. After flipping through a few racks, she grabs a light blue dress and another one in a soft yellow color. After less than five minutes in the dressing room, she comes back out holding the blue one.

"I'll take this one and those nude sandals in a size seven."

While the saleslady collects the shoes, Seven grabs one of those little sparkly purses girls always carry to fancy events and then plucks a pair of earrings off the display on the counter. A few minutes later, we're outside in the sunshine.

"That was the fastest shopping trip I've ever been on. My mom used to take forever picking out a dress."

Seven throws her bag in the backseat of my car and then climbs in the front. "Your mom is gorgeous and probably knows how to dress. I just try to look appropriate and fit in. Fashion isn't my thing and never will be so I stick to the same basic colors. Blue usually works. Besides, no one will be looking at me."

There's no anger or sadness in the statement. Instead she says it as a matter of fact, like it should be obvious to everyone. I open my mouth to say something but she's already turned toward the window.

Once we get back to my apartment, she makes an excuse about needing to work and then disappears into the guest room. I let out a sigh. I should have said something. It kills me that she sees herself that way, as unattractive or unworthy. Her scar bothers her, I can tell by the way she hides it, but I barely see it now. I noticed it when we first met but now it's just part of her face like the shape of her eyes or the curve of her lush bottom lip.

Disturbed by the direction of my thoughts, I sit on the couch and bury myself in my own work. The next time I look up, it's after lunchtime.

Shit. The wedding starts in two hours and as a groomsman I'm supposed to arrive early so we can take pictures. That's probably something I should have mentioned to Seven when I asked her to come with me. Most women appreciate a little time to get ready before an event.

"Sev, it's time to get ready," I call out.

I don't hear any movement so I close my laptop and then walk down the hall. I knock on the door once, then again before opening it slightly. There's a muffled curse and when I open the door all the way, I see why.

Seven is in the middle of pulling her dress over her head.

We both freeze and the sight of her slim curves in the sheerest bra and panties I've ever seen is instantly burned into my brain. There's a warning sound going off in the back of my mind telling me that I should turn around to give her privacy. That I'm being an asshole by standing here staring at her while she's struggling to pull her dress down.

But I can't move.

Her dusky nipples are clearly visible through the sheer material of her bra and behind the front panel of her bikini bottoms, I can tell that she's completely bare. My mouth falls open but all that comes out is a little wheezing sound.

Completely. Bare.

"Oh Jesus."

"Oh my god."

We speak at the same time. Seven finally turns around to face the window but of course that doesn't help much. Now I'm presented with the elegant line of her spine and also with the evidence that what I thought was a bikini panty is in fact a thong.

"Fucking hell."

"*Luke!*"

"I'm sorry. Fuck." I close the door and then lean my head against it. My hand clenches around the doorknob. It's taking all my self-control not to open the door and go back in that room.

I hear another muffled curse from behind the door.

"Sev? Are you okay?"

It's quiet for a moment then I hear, "I'm stuck."

"What?"

"Oh just open the door, damn it."

I push open the door again. She's still facing away from me and I clench my jaw when I get another look at her curvy little ass. I wouldn't have expected her to have such a round bottom when she's so thin but her clothes have been hiding a gorgeous shape.

"When you're done staring at my ass could you *help* me?"

Her angry words pull me out of my stupor. While I've been standing here ogling her, she's still got her arms stuck over her head, trapped by the dress.

"Sorry. Here, just hold still." I manage to pull the dress up slightly so she can get her arms out of it.

Once she's free, she rubs her shoulders. "Thanks, the damn thing was strangling me."

Now that she's standing normally, it's even harder to keep my eyes on her face. When our eyes meet, she blushes again. Her hand goes up to brush her hair forward over the scarred side of her face. That one movement just about breaks me. Just the idea that she could be worried about how she looks in front of me ...

I pull her against me until we fit together from chest to thigh. She sucks in a sharp breath and her hands land on my chest.

"Luke, what are you doing?"

"Hell if I know."

Then I'm kissing her. No longer caring about taking things slow or whether I can trust her, in that moment I'm acting purely on instinct. She shudders against me and her lips part, hot and needy against mine. *Finally.* I don't waste any more time waiting for permission before my tongue seeks out hers, teasing her with gentle strokes.

Her fingers flex against my chest and the gentle pressure feels so damn good. I've never been more conscious of the difference in our sizes but the way she's clutching at me makes me want to curl my whole body around her. To protect her and shelter her. Her head falls back and my mouth follows the line of her throat before coming back up to take her lips again. I love the way she tastes, slightly sweet like she's been eating candy.

"Luke?"

Her voice startles me, pulling me out of the haze I've slipped into. When I open my eyes, she's staring up at me plaintively. That's when I realize I'm holding her under the arms so tightly that she can't move. Her dress is crumpled between us. I immediately let go and she steps back.

"I am so sorry."

"You don't have to—"

"Yes, I do. I'll wait outside so you can get dressed." I don't look at her again, just walk to the door.

But just before I close it, I turn around. She's still standing by the window holding her dress in front of her like a shield. Her hair has been mussed by my hands and there's a sexy, satisfied little smile on her face. I can't deny the intense satisfaction I get from knowing I made her look like that.

"Plenty of people will be looking at you tonight, Sev. Especially me."

———

After changing into the tuxedo Tank convinced me it was smarter to buy than rent, we drive over to the restaurant. Seven is extremely quiet in the car and I can't think of anything to break the silence. Clearly I can't be trusted not to say something inappropriate after my earlier behavior.

Even though she said I didn't have to apologize, it's obvious that I scared her a little. She looked completely unnerved standing there holding her dress like it could protect her from me. I practically mauled the girl and she's so tiny she couldn't push me off.

The restaurant has a sign that it's closed for a private event but the door is open. We follow the flower trails out to the back. Everything was pretty much set up last night but now the large grassy lawn behind the restaurant has been completely transformed into an oasis of white and pink flowers. As soon as you walk outside, there's a little table with the guestbook so I sign in for both of us.

"I have to go find Tank and the other guys. Are you going to be okay on your own?"

Seven nods a little too quickly. When her eyes finally meet mine, the tops of her cheeks turn pink. "You told them I'm coming, right?"

"Yeah, Tank said it was fine. He put you in the second row so you'll be right up front."

She nods. "Go on, be with your brothers. I'll be fine."

I want to say something but I can't think of anything other than "*I like the way your lips feel*" so I just watch helplessly as an usher escorts Seven to her seat in the second row, right behind Tank's mother. Once my mom arrives, she'll be seated on the same row. Mom will have plenty of time to interrogate Seven tonight, unfortunately. I'll be stuck taking pictures after the ceremony for at least a half an hour.

I walk towards the hallway and almost bump into Gabe. He looks relieved when he sees me.

"Glad you're here. Tank is about to hyperventilate."

"What?" I follow him to a room I didn't see last night. Tank is pacing in front of a mirror, wearing a tuxedo minus the jacket. His hair is sticking straight up and his eyes are wild. Finn is talking to him in a low voice.

Zack jumps up when we enter. "Dude, where have you been? He's about to crawl out the window. I thought we were going to have to restrain him. I'm sure you can guess about how well that would go."

He glances over at Tank and we take a collective breath. Tank is aptly nicknamed and if he freaks out it'll probably take all four of us to hold him down.

"What the hell is going on?"

Gabe hands me a maroon cummerbund and a bow tie. It's been a really long time since I've tied one of these but I manage to get it into a decent shape.

"He thinks that Emma wants to back out of the wedding for some reason. Finn has been trying to calm him down. Nothing has been working."

Zack yanks at his own bowtie until Gabe finally slaps his hand away and ties it for him.

I look over at Tank again. His expression reminds me of how he looked at his bachelor party. Then I remember Seven's words when I told her about Tank's drunken whining.

All he wants is her.

"I have an idea but I'm not sure it'll work. And it's risky. Where are the girls?"

Gabe leans out the door and points down the hallway. "The room at the end of the hall."

"Try to keep him calm."

I jog down the hall and knock on the door. It opens and a cloud of perfume and giggles comes out. Sasha looks surprised to see me. Josie peeks over her shoulder and takes my picture.

"Luke, what are you doing here? I thought you were the other photographer. If you see him, tell him to hurry up. Josie can't take pictures while she's walking down the aisle—"

"No, that's not why I'm here. Sorry to interrupt but I need to talk to Emma for a second."

The girls move back and then I can see Emma standing in front of the mirror. Like most guys my age, I haven't thought too much about marriage except as a thing to do someday. But even I can't deny that Emma is a vision. Under her veil, her blond hair is twisted up into an elegant knot. Her white dress nips in at the waist and then billows in layers that make her look like a princess.

"Wow. You are gorgeous."

She flushes adorably at the compliment. "Thank you, Luke."

"I have a favor to ask. And I know it's probably completely against the wedding rules."

She holds out her hands to me and I cross the room, dodging kicked off high heels and what looks like lingerie.

"What's going on? Is Tank okay?"

"No. He's not. That's why I need a favor. I need you to kiss him before the wedding."

Emma is already shaking her head. "It's bad luck to see the groom before the wedding."

"There might not be a wedding if he runs out of here!"

Emma looks stricken and a girl with dark, wavy hair puts her arm around her and gives me a nasty look. "Tank wouldn't do that. Stop scaring my sister!"

Sasha grabs my arm. "Is it really that bad?"

I'm suddenly surrounded by a sea of worried faces. *Okay, Luke. Maybe this wasn't the best plan.* It wasn't my intention to scare the hell out of Emma on her wedding day but I've seen Tank when he freaks out. It's not a pretty sight. I take a deep breath. Talking about it isn't going to get the job done here. If Emma could see how bad Tank looks right now, she'd know I'm right.

I pull out my phone and call Zack. He answers immediately.

"Blindfold Tank. I'm bringing Emma to you guys." Then I hang up.

"You're doing what?"

"Where are you taking her?"

The room explodes into a chorus of worried questions as I grab Emma's hand and tug her toward the door. She follows me into the hall, Sasha and Josie scrambling behind her to carry the train of her dress. Zack peeks his head out of the door and his eyes go wide when he sees me leading a charge of women down the hall.

"This is your plan?" he hisses.

I push him out of the way. "Do you have a better idea?"

Zack moves back to let us inside. As soon as Emma sees Tank across the room she drops my hand and runs to him. He has what looks like a tie around his eyes but even with half his face covered you can tell he's a nervous wreck. As soon as

Emma wraps her arms around him, his whole body shudders in relief.

"Emma, you're still here."

"Of course I'm still here. Didn't I tell you I would never leave you?" she whispers back.

"Come on, everybody. Let's give them some privacy." Sasha shoos us all out the door. We all stand in the hall awkwardly trying not to listen too closely to the soft voices coming from behind the door.

After a few minutes, Emma emerges wiping tears from her eyes. "Everything is okay now. Thank you for getting me, Luke."

I let out a sigh of relief. "I did the right thing? No bad luck?"

Emma smiles and hugs me. "No bad luck. Thank you, little brother."

We watch as she leads the girls back down the hall. Once they're gone, we go back in the room. Tank is looking out the window with the most peaceful expression on his face.

"Is everything okay?" I ask tentatively.

Tank turns and then picks up his jacket. He shrugs into it and then moves to the mirror to adjust his bowtie.

"Everything is more than okay. Now where the hell is that photographer so we can get these pictures out of the way."

He catches my eye in the reflection and mouths *thank you*. Then he turns around.

"Let's get this show on the road. I'm ready to get hitched."

Chapter Ten

Seven

Some people are weddings people. They love flowers and cake, puffy dresses and vows of forever. They cry at the idea of people pledging their troth and swoon at the exchange of rings. They're in love with the idea of love.

I have *never* been one of those people.

But as I watch Tank standing at the end of the aisle flanked by his four brothers, I can't remain unmoved by it all. He looks so excited, his eyes trained on the door where his bride will appear. Then the bridal march starts and he gets his first look at her walking down the aisle toward him. He looks like every dream he's ever had just came true. Emma looks much the same, absolutely glowing with her love for him.

When she reaches him, Tank steps down from the altar to take her hands and then gives her a little kiss to the consternation of the minister. As he coughs in disapproval, a titter of laughter goes through the crowd. They both look so unapologetic about it that even I want to sigh a little.

I can't deny that it almost makes me a believer. Almost. But then I've always known that love is out there for the lucky few who can find it.

I've just never been that lucky.

My eyes immediately seek out Luke. My breath catches when I find that he's been watching *me*.

Of course my imagination does the unthinkable and immediately produces an image of the two of us standing before a preacher glowing with love and excitement. Just as quickly, I shut that down.

I have no right to dream about forever with Luke when I've been plotting against him this whole time. The thought of it makes me feel ashamed so I don't look at him again.

The rest of the ceremony proceeds smoothly and when the minister finally says *You may kiss the bride*, Tank wastes no time. The crowd is on their feet cheering when they finally break the passionate kiss and they're both wiping tears away as they walk back down the aisle hand in hand. I wait patiently for the bridesmaids and groomsmen to file out before making my way through the crowd looking for Luke.

"Seven!"

When I see him waving at me, I dodge a few people to get across the room.

"Hey! We have to take a few more pictures and then we can relax a bit. There's food out already and it's open bar so hopefully you won't be too bored waiting for me. I'm sorry—"

I put a finger over his lips to silence him. "Why do you keep apologizing?"

"You know why." He lowers his voice and glances around him to make sure no one can hear us. "I practically assaulted you before we came here."

Is that how he sees what happened? Our version of events definitely don't match up because I thought it was the single hottest thing that's ever happened to me.

"What are you talking about? Luke ... I liked it. *Really* liked it."

He moves closer. "You did?"

"Yeah." It comes out as a rush of breath, sounding way more breathy and sexy than I intended.

"Good. So did I. I'm sure you could tell." The corner of his mouth lifts. "Now I really don't want to go. Anyway, my mom is here. I saw her come in right before the ceremony started. I apologize in advance if she asks you to marry me and have my babies before I get back."

He looks so worried that I can't help laughing. "We'll be fine. If nothing else, I'll get drunk and tell her sad stories of growing up without a mother. I'm sure that'll cure her desire to have me in the family."

"That won't matter to her. And it doesn't matter to me either." He taps me on the nose softly and the affectionate gesture takes me off guard.

"Okay, see you later."

I watch as he melts into the crowd and then move toward the bar. If I'm going to survive a night with Luke's sudden intensity and questioning by a concerned mom, I'll need a drink in me first.

I'm just taking a sip of a vodka tonic when Anita appears at my elbow and asks the bartender for a martini.

"There you are, honey! I got here a little late so I didn't get to say hi to you before the ceremony started."

"Oh hello again, Ms. Marshall. It was a beautiful wedding, wasn't it?"

Usually it's just something you say at weddings but this time, I mean it. Watching two people that genuinely excited to be together *was* beautiful.

"It really was. It's been a real joy to get to know Tank and Emma. They're very fond of Luke."

There's something wistful in the way she says it that makes me think. It has to be hard for her to be here surrounded by all her son's half-brothers. All the evidence that a man she once loved couldn't be faithful.

Suddenly I don't want to tell her all the bad things about me hoping to scare her off.

"Luke is very fond of you. As long as we've been friends, that's the one thing I've always known."

"How long is that?" she asks curiously.

"Um, more than ten years now."

She smiles in delight. "Is that right? Well, then I have to thank you for being such a good friend to him. All this time he's told me that his online friendships are real and true. I couldn't really understand it before but now that I've met you, I do. I understand exactly why my son has treasured his friendship with you for so long. You have a good heart, honey. I can tell."

"You can?"

I desperately want to believe her. I'm constantly conflicted about the choices I should make and I never feel like any of them are the right ones. I want to believe that she can see something in me that I can't in myself.

She pats my hand. "Yes. Now let me tell you about what a good husband my son would make."

Her switch into matchmaker mode comes so quickly and so smoothly that I have to acknowledge it with a little bow. "Luke warned me that you'd be measuring me for a wedding dress."

She chuckles. "You can't blame a mother for trying. Now tell me about yourself. What do you do? Is it the same thing Luke does or something else I won't really be able to understand?"

Laughing, I pull out my phone. "I'm in cyber security but I also design video games. Let me show you one of my best-sellers. This is called *Pig Punt*."

By the time Luke finds us a half hour later, Anita has down-loaded the game on her own phone, is on level five and we've officially become friends. He looks over his mom's shoulder and his brow crinkles in disbelief when he sees what she's doing.

"Mom, are you playing a game? I didn't know you even knew how to download games on your phone."

Anita lets out a whoop. "Level Six baby! I didn't know how. Seven showed me. Luke, why didn't you tell me these games were so much fun? I kicked that little piggy right over the barn!"

Luke turns to me. "Who is this woman you're trying to pass off as my mother?"

Anita gives him a smug smile. "You don't know all my secrets yet, young man. Remember that, Seven. You have to keep them guessing."

I laugh at the befuddled look on Luke's face. "Yes, ma'am. I'll remember that."

"Okay, I have no idea what just happened but I've been waiting for this all night. Dance with me." He holds out his hand.

I glance over at Anita, hesitant to leave her alone. She shakes her head and waves us off. "Go. Go! Dance while you're young and can do all those crazy moves."

Laughing, I accept Luke's hand. "I don't know any crazy moves but I'll just fake it 'til I make it, I guess."

He pulls me closer until I fit right in the cradle of his arms. Then he bends his head until his lips are at my ear. "There won't be any faking between us. Believe that."

I bury my face against his shoulder, ignoring his chuckles. He seems to enjoy making me blush. The song is a fast number but we're slow dancing for some reason. Luke doesn't seem to care though and neither do I. Finally the music changes to a slow song and his arm slips lower on my back, holding me against him.

"Tell me something about you. Something I don't know," he murmurs in my ear.

This is a hard one. We've talked about so many things over the years. He knew I was in foster care and that I have a younger sister. I've told him about my social anxiety and how hard it is to make friends.

"I want to, I just don't know where to start."

He tilts his head. "What about your name? You use the number seven in your alias too so I assume it must have a special significance."

My hand clenches against his shoulder. Of all the things he would ask me, this is the one question I should have expected. But thinking about it always takes me off guard.

"It's okay if you don't want to."

"No, it's not that. I'm just trying to figure out how to explain it."

I watch the other dancers swirling around us. We're surrounded by happy couples. This would usually make me feel my solitude even more acutely but for the first time, I feel like I'm one of them.

Being with Luke makes me feel like I belong.

"I was seven years old when my mother decided she couldn't take care of us anymore. Grace was only a few months old. She told me we were going out for ice cream."

Luke rests his head on top of mine. Even without seeing his eyes, I can feel his horror in the way his arm tightens around me.

"I didn't know you were so young when it happened," he says finally.

"All I remember of her is that she had dark hair like mine and she always smelled like apples. Even though I can't see her face anymore, I remember clinging to her while she was trying to leave. I just kept saying *I'll be good. I'll be a good girl, I promise.*" My voice breaks and suddenly his other arm is around me too and he's hugging me right there on the dance floor.

"It was nothing you did, baby. I hope you know that."

Tucking my head, I wipe beneath my eyes, hoping no one has noticed that I'm crying in the middle of the dance floor.

"I do know that. It took a while but ... yeah."

After a few moments of swaying silently, I clear my throat. "Anyway, for months after that everyone I met would ask me two questions. What's your name? And how old are you? It became an automatic thing to answer *I'm Sarah. I'm seven.* Over and over. Even at that young age I knew that all those people weren't really interested in me. They were just doing their jobs. To them I was just a number."

I pull back and look up at him. His eyes are shiny with unshed tears as he smiles gently down at me.

"That's why it's your personal number, isn't it? Because that's how old you were when your life changed."

"No, it's how old I was when I learned that I was *on my own.*"

A tear slides down his cheek. Moved, I reach up to wipe it away. Then right there in front of everyone, he kisses me again.

Unlike before, it's not a frenzied rush of emotion with searching hands and tongues but a gentle kiss. A sweet kiss. Nothing he could have done would have made me feel more cherished.

And it completely freaks me out.

"Excuse me, I need to ... I need to use the bathroom."

I can feel Luke's eyes on me as I push through the crowd looking for an exit. Any exit will do even if it leads to the parking lot. I just can't stay in this room with Luke, his adorable mom and the promise of happiness any longer.

Chapter Eleven

Seven

In a stroke of luck, the first door I find actually does lead to a bathroom. There's only one person in there so I'm able to close myself into a stall until I catch my breath.

Even though I've had a crush on him for years, falling in love wasn't part of my plan. Love is one of those things reserved for the lucky few, a privileged class I could only observe from a distance. This isn't my life. Things like this don't happen to me. I don't belong here in his perfect, ordered world.

But it's starting to feel like I could and that scares the hell out of me. I can visualize it completely and the wanting hurts more than anything else.

Wanting something I'll never have is unbearable.

I pull out my phone and then tap my code to unlock it. I have a text message from Grace. I check the time before calling her back. Her foster parents are used to her gabbing in her room at night to friends so I try to only call her then. Not that the Barnetts aren't nice but I don't want to give them any reason to try to keep us apart. I figure the less they know about how much contact we have, the better.

Once I hear the bathroom door close and I know I'm alone, I call. Grace answers on the second ring but I can barely hear her over the loud music she's playing.

"Are you blasting your stereo again? Didn't you get in trouble for that last week?"

The volume of the music lowers slightly. "Whatever. I'm already in trouble anyway. Again."

My heart sinks. "What did you do now?"

There's an indignant huff on the other end of the line. "I *may* have gotten in trouble at school for kneeing a dude. In the junk."

"Ouch. But I'm sure you wouldn't have done that without a reason. Did this boy put his hands on you?"

This is why I'm so determined to get Grace out of the system. To those people you're nothing but a number and few people care enough to advocate for you.

I didn't have anyone to stand for me but I'm determined to be that for Grace.

"Calm down, momma bear. He just popped my bra strap." She sounds so disgusted that I can actually picture her rolling her eyes.

"Boys still do that? Seriously?" Now that I'm not worried about her being in actual harm's way, it's easy to see the absurdity of it.

"This one won't be doing it again," she drawls smugly.

"Yeah, I bet. So why did you get in trouble when he did something to you first?"

"Something about not retaliating with violence, *blah, blah*. I wasn't really listening to that part."

"Grace. I'm doing everything I can to get you out of there but you have to behave."

"I'm behaving. Everyone around me is the problem. So where are you? I called you a bunch of times."

There's a loud crunching sound like she's eating junk food while she's talking to me. It gives me such a great mental image of her, curled up on her bed snacking while she's supposed to be grounded. Enjoying herself even when she's technically in trouble. That's typical Grace. My little rebel.

"Oh, I'm ... not in New York."

"Where are you then? You never go anywhere."

I've told her about Luke before and she knows that I've been crushing on him for years. If I tell her where I am, she'll know why I'm here. I sigh.

"I'm in Virginia. Visiting Luke."

"*What?* You finally got up the nerve to do it? Oh my god this is so exciting! What is he like? Does he like you? *Have you kissed him yet?*"

Her excitement is contagious and before long I'm giggling like a teenage girl, too. My sister is the only person that brings out this side of me. Other than Luke, that is. I've been doing my fair share of giggling around him this past week.

"Slow down. I'm here working with him on a project."

Grace makes a snorting sound. "Project? Sounds boring. You've been talking about this guy for so long I was pretty sure he was your imaginary friend. Now you're there visiting? Come on Seven, I'm not a baby. I know why you're really there."

Even though she can't see me, I can feel the heat climbing to my face. "We *are* working on a project, I'll have you know. He asked me to help him start a technology program for underprivileged kids."

"Hmm. Well if you're just working together that must mean he's not attractive in real life. *Bummer*." My pause seems to give her the answer she's looking for. "Hah, I knew it. He's hot, isn't he?"

"He's very good-looking," I admit.

"Is he now? Cute for a geeky guy or like really sexy? Because there's a difference."

"He's gorgeous." I give up trying to play it cool. "Everything I ever imagined and more."

Grace squeals on the other end of the phone. "Are you at his house? Why are you calling me? You should be doing sexy stuff right now. Then you can tell me all about it!"

"I won't be telling you anything about that," I splutter. Grace has always been the bold one and loves mortifying me by asking inappropriate questions. It's hard to believe she's seven years younger than I am.

"You're my big sister. Who else am I going to ask?"

"That's true. I'd rather you ask me than your friends who will definitely give you bad advice."

"This is your chance to find out if the online connection can be more than that. Don't waste it!"

"I'm not wasting anything. I'm just worried about you."

"Worry about the hottie hacker instead of me. Figure out a way to infiltrate his systems or whatever you nerds call it."

"Brat."

"I'm serious, Seven. You always worry about me. Well, now I'm worried about you. You have a chance to hang out with a cool guy who totally gets you and you're on the phone with me instead. What's wrong with this picture?"

I lean against the door of the stall, suddenly really depressed. "When did you get so wise? Aren't you supposed to be a moody teenager who wears too much eye makeup and listens to boy bands?"

"Stop trying to change the subject. I'm serious here. You always take care of me but who takes care of you? Maybe this Luke guy would if you'd let him."

"I don't know ... He seems to like me too, but you know I'm not good at this kind of thing. Maybe I'm reading it all wrong. He probably has some supermodel girlfriend that I just haven't run into yet."

Grace is quiet. Even though I've never said it directly, she knows how self-conscious I am about the scar on my face even though she doesn't know how I got it. That isn't something I talk about.

"Well, I'll tell you what. Step one is to stop talking to me and go jump his bones."

"Grace! I'm pretty sure jumping someone isn't step one." But she's accomplished what she meant to. I'm no longer feeling sad and pitiful.

"If it isn't step one, it should be. Life is short."

"Oh the wisdom of fifteen. How I miss it. Go do some homework or contemplate who's hotter, Harry or Nevin."

"Wow, Sev. Not that I'm into pop music but at least I can get their names right."

We're both still laughing when we hang up.

———

After I splash my face with water, I venture back out onto the dance floor. Now that I've calmed down a little, I'm embarrassed by the way I ran out. I just ditched Luke and left him with no explanation. He probably thinks I'm crazy.

Anita isn't standing by the bar anymore and I don't see anyone else I recognize. My usual insecurity comes back and

I suddenly feel really exposed standing in the middle of the floor by myself. Just when I'm about to turn around and go back to hiding out in the bathroom, I bump into someone.

"Seven?"

I turn at the sound of my name. It's one of the bridesmaids, a gorgeous girl with brown skin and long curly hair.

"You're Luke's girlfriend, right?" Before I have a chance to confirm or deny, she has me by the hand. I follow dumbly as she leads me into the center of a group of chattering women.

"Look who I found girls. It's Luke's girlfriend. This is Seven everybody!"

Oh god. Just kill me now. This is exactly like a recurring nightmare I have, being pulled into a big group of people and then having everyone stare at me.

"Hi!"

"Oh it's nice to meet you!"

I can barely keep up with everyone's name and I'm hugged more times than I can keep track of. Eventually I end up at a table where the other bridesmaids are sitting and someone pushes a glass of champagne into my hand.

"Hi, I'm Josie. I'm Zack's girlfriend. Sasha is the one who dragged you over here. She's engaged to Gabe. And that's

Finn's wife, Rissa." She points at a redhead who is talking to Emma.

"My head is spinning."

Josie laughs. "I know the feeling. Trust me, you'll get used to it."

Rissa takes a seat next to me and before I know it, I'm pulled into their conversation about the honeymoon. Rissa gets up to check something and Emma moves closer to me.

"We're all so thrilled to meet you. Luke is so brilliant and kind of mysterious in a way. None of us even knew he had a girlfriend."

Sasha brings her another glass of champagne. Emma takes it with a tight smile. Beneath the table, her hand goes to her stomach.

She's pregnant. And no one else knows.

When everyone else is occupied, I switch my empty glass with Emma's full one. Her eyes lift to mine.

"It's okay. I can keep a secret."

She lets out a breath. "Did I mention how glad I am that Luke brought you?"

"You don't have to say that to get me to stick around. I'm just here for the free champagne."

She smiles gratefully. "Thank you."

Over the next hour, I'm pulled into a variety of conversations. Emma tells me more about the honeymoon she and Tank are taking to St. Thomas. Sasha invites me to her next performance at a jazz lounge in Virginia Beach and Josie shows me pictures on her cell phone from her last art gallery showing.

The entire time I'm amazed by how friendly they all are. They don't even know me and they've taken me in as one of their own. It's the nicest thing anyone has ever done for me but also makes me feel worse than ever.

It makes me wish that this was all real.

"Why are you all being so nice to me? You don't even know me," I finally ask.

"You're Luke's girlfriend. Why wouldn't we be nice to you? The guys spend so much time together that we end up spending time together too. We're all going to be sisters-in-law eventually." Emma squeezes my hand.

"That's just it. I'm not really his girlfriend. We're ... friends."

Sasha winks. "Well, we may not know you yet but we know Luke. And we've *never* seen him like this."

Her eyes shift over my shoulder and I turn around. Luke is on the other side of the room talking to his brothers. Even though they're all standing in a circle, there's a distance between them, as if he's separate somehow. Now that I know him better, I can tell that he's a little uncomfortable.

He laughs and then his eyes meet mine and his expression changes. He bites his lip and I can read what he's thinking from across the room. That he wants to bite me instead.

Wowza.

I feel my face flush as the other girls giggle behind me. When I turn around, Sasha gives me a pointed look.

"Friends, huh?"

"We are," I insist, although I'm sure the blush in my cheeks is undermining my authority in this case.

"Look at how he's looking at you. Girl, he looks like he could just eat you up. Maybe you should let him." She hums suggestively and then grabs another champagne flute off the tray of a passing waiter.

"Here, you look like you could use a little liquid courage."

I accept the glass but only so she won't give it to someone else. Namely, Emma. Champagne isn't my favorite thing but this stuff tastes way better than the cheap bottle I got myself for New Year's.

Hesitantly, I take a sip. Usually I don't drink much so I've been trying to pace myself. It's refreshing and a little tingly in my mouth. Maybe I do like champagne after all.

"Drink up," Sasha urges. "Maybe enough of that can take you and Luke from friends to lovers."

"You're so bad. Ignore her," Josie tells me.

Sasha preens, clearly taking it as a compliment.

"Hey, I'm only trying to help Luke out! We want you to stick around." Sasha clinks her glass against mine.

In the middle of that giggling group of women, I have never felt more welcome.

Or like more of a fraud.

Chapter Twelve

Luke

"We made it. Thanks to you."

Tank raises his beer in my direction and the other guys follow suit.

"I seriously hope we got pictures of that. You looked so cute with your blindfold on." Zack jumps back before Tank can reach him.

Always the mediator, Finn steps in between them. "Women stress out about weddings. I'm sure it had nothing to do with you. Emma loves you and that's what matters. All you have to do is focus on giving her the perfect honeymoon."

Just as a matter of principle, I make a retching sound. That breaks up the tension and we all laugh.

Zack crosses his arms and stares at me. "You're always giving us a hard time about being whipped but word on the street is that you're no longer single either."

I glare at Tank who doesn't look even slightly sorry for ratting me out. "Snitch."

"Oh come on, you knew I was going to tell them."

Finn makes a face. "Why am I always the last to hear everything?"

As much as I love annoying them about their women, it's not so easy to be on the other end of the scrutiny. Especially since I'm not exactly sure what's going on between me and Seven. We're not together but we're not strictly friends either, are we?

And considering how she ran away right after I kissed her, she's feeling just as conflicted as I am. I shouldn't have pushed her to talk about her past.

"It's not a big deal. Seven is staying with me for a while. Tank happened to meet her the other day when he was at the bakery. She's a friend from out of town."

"A very pretty friend," Tank adds.

Zack makes kissing noises. It's so immature yet so funny that I can't help laughing.

"Oh wow. And you guys are supposed to be my older brothers? Are we really sure about that?"

He shoves me. "With that baby face, is there really any doubt?"

Gabe comes back from the bar and hands out beers. He offers me one but I shake my head. I'll need to drive home in about an hour so I've already cut myself off.

"I'm just going to keep 'em coming. I can't believe you're married now," he says to Tank. "Another one bites the dust. Sasha and I are up next unless Josie convinces you to elope, Zack."

At the panicked look on Zack's face, I'm guessing that won't be happening.

"Technically I guess I have to propose first," he replies.

Gabe looks disgusted. "You still haven't asked her? After everything you went through to be with her, what are you waiting for?"

"The perfect moment." Zack crosses his arms. "She knows I want to be with her forever. But I've only got one chance to ask her and I have to get this right."

"However you ask her will be perfect. She won't care about whether it's on a billboard or during a hot air balloon ride. If it was me, I would just ask her one day over coffee. Take her completely by surprise."

The image of getting down on one knee next to Seven after breakfast one day is so clear in my mind it's almost like a memory. Or a vision of what's to come. I smile thinking about how shocked she'd be if I actually did that one day. I love seeing that look on her face, when she's surprised or delighted by something.

"You seem to have given this some thought," Tank says.

I regret thinking out loud when I notice the others exchanging glances. "That doesn't mean I'm getting married any time soon. I'm just saying."

"Is your friend the reason behind this sudden change of heart?" Finn asks.

He's just teasing, I can tell by the twinkle in his eye, but I answer seriously anyway.

"Maybe. I'm seeing a lot of things differently since she came around."

Tank takes another long pull on his beer. "The right woman will do that to you. I know I was a wreck earlier but that's because I was nervous about screwing up Em's perfect wedding. Was I nervous about marrying her? Not at all."

His candid answer is a little unnerving. What is it like to trust someone so completely? There's so much about Seven that I still don't know and even though I want to trust her, all my instincts are telling me that something isn't right.

There's something going on with her and I have to figure out what it is.

"Is everything okay, Luke?"

All eyes swing to me and I squirm under the scrutiny. At least it's just my brothers. The girls have long ago abandoned us and are clustered at one of the tables *oohing* and *aahing* over something Josie is showing them on her camera.

"You know you can talk to us if you need to."

Zack nudges me in the side. "Come on, I'm sorry for razzing you earlier. It's all in fun."

Having people to confide in isn't something I'm used to but I find myself ready to take a chance. I do need advice and my brothers are exactly the kind of guys who would understand.

I shake my head. "No, it's not that. It's just ... Have you ever liked someone, a girl, you weren't sure you could trust?"

Tank leans forward. "You don't trust your friend? Why?"

Of course he narrows in on the real deal right away. That's Tank for you. He gets right to the point and doesn't suffer bullshit. But maybe that's exactly what I need right now. I've been dancing around the problem, too afraid to examine why I don't trust Seven yet. It's more than just her weird behavior this afternoon. It's a gut feeling that I can't explain.

"Yeah. I didn't tell you the whole story that day when you met her. The reason the FBI came and got me that day was because of her."

While I briefly summarize the entire meeting with Agent Walker and everything that happened after, Tank listens intently. Then he holds up a hand.

"Hold on. You said you went to the hotel and got her laptop and suitcase, right?"

"Yeah. That was all she brought with her."

He narrows his eyes. "But I thought you said she was busted by the FBI for hacking into something?"

"Yeah, she was."

"If she was hacking into something, wasn't she using her computer then?"

I open my mouth to reply and then shut it just as quickly. "Which would mean that her laptop would still be in FBI custody."

Finn and the other guys look confused as hell. Finally Zack asks, "What does that mean?"

I glance at him and then back to Tank who nods slowly.

"It means that my instincts are right. She's lying to me."

———

The rest of the guys are dancing and Seven appears to be having a good time with Sasha and the girls. I'm surprised to see her socializing so easily since I know that's hard for her. But then again Sasha has a way of making everyone feel comfortable.

It's so strange now to look back at how tongue-tied I used to be around her. When we first met, I had a huge crush on her but now I just see Gabe's girl. My future sister-in-law. Then I look over at Seven and I see all these possibilities. Even though I know she's not telling me the whole truth, I just can't believe that she's actually trying to hurt me. My gut is telling me she's being pushed into something against her will. I just don't know why.

Yet.

I leave the main dining room and wander back down the hall to the rooms where we got dressed. This restaurant is set up with several lounge areas which is great when you need a bit of quiet to think. The only information I have to work with here is that Seven's story of being arrested by the FBI doesn't make sense. Thinking back on that day, I puzzle over how that could be true. Agent Walker himself is the one who told me she was arrested.

Agent Walker.

"Son of a bitch."

I stand, pacing as the pieces of a theory start to come together. Agent Walker came into my life not just because I was accused of something but because he needed me. He needed my skills to help him close his cases. He's not a bad guy but he's all about the bottom line. His goal is to get information and he'll use anything or anyone he has to in order to accomplish that.

When my father first came back into my life, Agent Walker asked if I'd had any contact with him and what I knew about him. I told him that I'd never even met my father before. I could tell he didn't believe me.

Due to my skills, he was probably assuming that I'd dig into my father's background and find all the dirt for them and then just hand it over. When that didn't happen, he wasn't happy about it but there wasn't anything he could do. He's tried to hack me before and failed every time.

I should have known he'd find a better way.

"Luke? What are you doing back here? You should be up front enjoying the party." Tank's mother takes a seat on one of the lounge chairs. She looks exhausted. I know she's been recovering from cancer.

"Yes, ma'am. I was just—" That's when I notice what's sticking out of the top of her bag. "Is that a laptop?"

She glances down. "Yes, isn't it cute? Tank just gave it to me last month."

"I hate to ask but I really need to check my email. Would you mind if I borrowed it? I'll bring it right back."

"Of course. Go right ahead." She hands it over and I take it to the couch across the room so I don't disturb her with my typing. It's a pretty basic model but I don't need much. I can log on to my server remotely and access whatever I need.

It's been a long time since I've done this but desperate times call for desperate measures. I pull up the last email I received from my father's assistant. I remember his bank's name from the legal paperwork so I quickly rip the html source from the legit site and use it to craft an official-looking email claiming she's been locked out of her bank access.

I modify the source to send any login credentials entered to one of my dummy websites. If she tries to click on anything other than the log in space, it won't work and she'll probably figure out that something is off. Hopefully she'll take the bait and I won't have to resort to more invasive methods to get her password. I close out of everything and delete the history before logging off.

"Here you go. Thank you." I put the laptop back in her bag.

Tank's mother nods and then closes her eyes again. I let myself out as quietly as possible.

I just broke who knows how many laws all because I have the vague idea that Seven's in trouble. I don't know what Agent Walker is holding over her head but I'm pretty sure he's using her against me in some way. I'm pissed that she didn't trust me enough to tell me so I could help her. But trust is something we can work on.

First, I need to give the FBI something they want so they'll leave her alone.

Chapter Thirteen

Luke

When I get back out to the main dining room, I can tell the reception is winding down a little. Apparently I missed the cake cutting, I observe as I pass the half-eaten wedding cake. I glance around looking for Seven. At least the crowd has thinned out a little. I just hope I haven't missed saying goodbye to Tank and Emma.

"There you are." Sasha loops her arm through mine and pulls me toward the front door. "Come on, the newlyweds are about to leave for the honeymoon."

We join everyone else out front where Tank and Emma stand next to a black Rolls Royce. A uniformed driver waits patiently holding the door open for them.

Emma sees me and comes over first. "Goodbye, Luke. Thank you again for what you did today. I'll never forget it." She hugs me and then moves down the line to hug Josie and Zack.

Tank appears next and we clasp hands before he pulls me into a one-armed hug. "Thanks for everything, bro. I'll see you guys in a few weeks. We'll have you and your lady over for dinner after we get back. Emma really likes her, by the way."

I finally notice Seven standing with the other bridesmaids, enveloped in a huge group hug with Emma at the center.

"I'm glad. I really like her, too."

There's a huge cheer from the crowd and suddenly everyone is throwing rice. Sasha pushes a small packet into my hands and I think, *what the hell*, and throw some rice, too.

We all wave as the car pulls away until the *Just Married* scrawled on the back is barely visible.

I wait patiently as everyone else goes back inside until I can get over to where Seven is standing alone. When she sees me, she breaks out into a huge grin and then practically jumps into my arms.

"Luke, there you are. I was looking all over for you. That was such a romantic wedding, wasn't it?"

She lets out a wistful sigh and drops her head on my shoulder. One of her legs is wrapped around my waist and she's almost climbing me. I can smell the sweet scent of the champagne she's been drinking on her breath. Just then she adjusts herself in my arms, rubbing right up against my groin. I get hard immediately.

"Had a few drinks, huh?" I shift around, trying to set her down gently but since her arms are locked around my neck, she ends up swaying against me. Basically lying on me while standing.

"Yeah. Usually I don't drink much but Sasha insisted that we have champagne to toast with and I had to take Emma's because she's pregnant. Did you know that?"

"No, I didn't but that explains quite a bit about today."

I lead her down the walkway to the parking lot. She's leaning against me with no abandon, her hand traveling under my jacket to rub up and down my back. *This is my punishment for some crime in a former life,* I think as one of her hands drops below my belt. Seven giggles when I jump, trying to keep her from discovering just how much my body is enjoying her champagne-fueled explorations. My sudden jerk seems to amuse her though because she lets out a happy little sigh and hooks her fingers in the waistband of my trousers.

"And then Josie wanted to get a picture of us with full champagne glasses so Emma gave me another one. Then Rissa insisted that I try the wine because it was her favorite. So before I knew it, I'd had at least three drinks. Your sisters-in-law are kind of pushy."

"Tell me about it."

By the time we get to my car, she's running her hands over my chest and rubbing her nose against my neck.

"Emma chose these boutonnieres because of the smell. Did you know that? She told me all about it. Everyone was so nice to me."

"I'm glad you had fun." I manage to juggle my keys out of my pocket and open the door.

"They all love each other. And they adore you." She peeks up at me, her face half hidden by her hair. "I adore you, too."

"Oh sweetheart, you are really killing me here."

I manage to get her in the car without incident but on the way home, she slides as close as she can get with her seatbelt on, resting her hand on my thigh. My hands tighten around the steering wheel and I have to check my natural impulse to drive faster.

By the time we arrive, she's nodded off.

I come around to her side of the car and scoop her into my arms. Her eyes open but she doesn't say anything. After how chatty she was earlier, she suddenly seems bashful again. I put her down briefly to open the door to my apartment but then pick her up again. There's no reason for me to do it. I'm just enjoying the excuse to have her this close.

I take her into my room and set her gently on the bed. Her eyes stay on mine, wide and waiting, as I pull down the zipper on the back of her dress. It's amazing how much louder a small sound like that seems in a dark room. She lifts up briefly and pushes the dress down to pool on the floor at her feet.

I pull her closer and kiss her gently on the forehead. "Good night, baby."

When I get up to leave, her arms lock around my neck almost strangling me. "Wait, where are you going to sleep?"

"I was going to take the futon," I stammer.

Without the barrier of her dress, her bra seems even sheerer than the last time I saw it. If I'm going to go, I need to leave now before I don't have enough blood left in my brain to make decisions. But before I can move, she swings a leg over my lap so she's straddling me.

"Don't do that. I want you to stay here. With me." Her hands tunnel through my hair and then her mouth is on mine.

"Sev, I don't want to do anything you're not ready for."

Moaning, she pulls back. "I'm not drunk, Luke. I'm a little tipsy, sure. But that's a good thing because otherwise I'd be too shy to do what I've been wanting to do all day."

She reaches behind her and unhooks her bra. It falls to the floor beside the bed. I watch it fall, feeling like it's taking my willpower with it.

When I look back at Seven, she looks so vulnerable. Almost like she's afraid that I won't like what I'm seeing. That fear in her eyes triggers every protective instinct I have. Nothing is more important than making sure she knows how beautiful she is to me and how honored I am to be with her right now.

"You're so beautiful. I'm almost scared to touch you."

She takes my hand and leads me to her breast. At the first brush of my hand against her nipple, she shudders and bites her lip.

"This is what I wanted you to do earlier today. I wanted you to touch me here. And here." She pulls my hand further down until I cup her through the sheer thong.

At the first touch, she cries out and bucks her hips. Seeing her so untamed snaps the last thread of my control. I hold her still, not allowing her to squirm away from the pleasure.

"Uh uh. Stay right there."

"*Luke.*" My name comes out as a plea.

"This is what you wanted, isn't it? You've been tormenting me all night with the memory of these." I take one of her tight little nipples in my mouth.

She pants as I suck it, hard. When I finally let it go with a little *pop*, it's dark red and so hard it could probably cut glass.

"Yes," she moans as my finger slides beneath her thong again.

"I can't get the image of this out of my head. Did you shave just to taunt me? Did you plan for me to see this so I'd be thinking about it all day?" My voice has deepened to a growl that I barely recognize.

"No. I didn't know..." She shudders above me as I pet the delicate skin, painting her moisture all over until one finger slides deep with ease. "Oh, that feels good."

I slide an arm up under her hair and hold her still. Finally, I have her where I want her and can do everything I've imagined. I don't plan on letting her go for hours.

With my other hand, I yank off my tie, then start working on the buttons on my shirt. Seven covers my hand with hers and unbuttons it the rest of the way. She pushes it and my jacket off my arms. When I settle us back on the bed, our skin meets for the first time and we both moan at the contact. She hooks her feet into the waistband of my pants and works them and my boxers over my hips. We're both smiling by the time they hit my ankles.

"Nice trick."

She raises her eyebrows. "They're in my way."

"We can't have that." I pull her legs around my hips and her back arches as I press against her again, this time with significantly less fabric between us.

My lips follow the line of her throat. Her hands grasp my hair, so tight it hurts, but the bite of pain is arousing. Her skin is slightly salty and I love the taste as I nip my way down to the gentle swell of her belly. She gasps again when I grab the edge of her thong with my teeth.

"This definitely needs to go."

Her soft sigh as I pull it down ramps my arousal higher. Hesitant to move too fast and shock her out of the moment, I trace her opening with my tongue, teasing her clit with little flicks. She shudders beneath me and when I look up, I'm shocked to see her eyes open, watching me. Her lids are heavy with desire and her bottom lip is clenched between her teeth.

While she watches, I brush my thumb up and down, teasing her little clit before pushing inside her gently.

Her mouth falls open and she cries out helplessly. The sound pushes me over the edge. I lean down, licking into her forcefully, letting her ride my tongue. Dimly, I'm aware of her cries and the flex of her fingers on my shoulders as she comes but I'm too far gone for finesse. I can't slow down when every instinct pushes me to tease her. Taste her.

Make her mine.

She's still gasping for breath when I reach over to the night table for protection. By the time I have a condom on, her eyes are open, watching my movements with interest. I gather her into my arms gently and then flip us over.

"I want you on top, baby. We'll take it as slow as you need to."

Although desire pushes me to take her, she's so tiny and I don't want to hurt her. She looks scared at first but then I brush my dick back and forth, using her moisture to smooth the way. She sighs and sinks down taking half of me before planting her hands on my chest.

A few deep breaths and then she rocks back and forth. It's so hard to hold still as she pulls me deeper and deeper into her tight grip but I keep my hands on her hips. When I finally hit bottom, her head falls back on her shoulder and she tightens around me.

"*Christ.* Do that again."

Her lashes flutter against her cheeks as she squeezes me again. Pleasure radiates through me as she raises up and then drops down again.

"Fuck, Sev. You feel amazing." I sit up against the backboard and the change in position makes us both groan. Her back arches so hard it looks like she'll bend in half and she squeezes around me over and over again.

"Damn baby, I feel you coming. Give it all to me."

I lift my hips, giving her the deep penetration I know she needs. She sobs, her fists falling against my chest as her orgasm rolls through her. My own pleasure beckons, trying to tempt me to follow her over the edge but I fight it. I'm not ready to let go yet.

But as I hover on that sharp edge of pleasure, it's the look in her eyes that takes me over. Like she's finally home.

Chapter Fourteen

Seven

Luke sits up all the way and somehow I'm on my back. He lowers himself on top of me, all without losing the connection between us. When he pulls out, I try not to flinch but he notices anyway. He kisses me softly.

"Poor baby. I'll take care of her in a minute."

He winks and climbs off the bed before disappearing into the hall. I hear the bathroom door close and that jolts me upright.

Frantically, I brush my hair down where it's sticking up in the back. After having a massive orgasm I should be relaxed but I'm suddenly extremely self-conscious. I've never lost complete control of myself like that before. I'm just glad Luke doesn't have a roommate because I don't think I could have been quiet to save my life.

He comes back and slides under the covers next to me. My eyes land on his cock which is still rock hard. I cover my mouth with my hand. *Damn.* When I look up at him, he's eyeing me with the most intense look on his face and I blush.

"Why are you looking at me like that?"

"Because now I know how good you feel. The things I was imagining before were pretty dirty but I wasn't even in the ballpark of how good it actually is."

He's nuzzling behind my ear as he says this and already my body is getting ready for him again. I clench my thighs, shocked by how achy and needy I feel down there.

Tentatively I reach out and place my hand in the center of his chest. He groans at the touch. Emboldened by the sound, I let myself stroke all the well-defined muscles in his abs. They flex under my fingers and I watch, fascinated at the sight. I bite my lip and then let my fingers drift a little lower.

"Fuck!"

He rears up and suddenly I have a fist full of him. He feels even bigger in my hand and I can hardly believe I took all of that inside. I've never been this bold with a guy before but with Luke I somehow know that no matter what I do it won't be wrong.

Nothing is off limits between us and that gives me the courage to explore. I brush my thumb over the slippery head, then again at his tortured moan.

"*Just like that*," he chokes out.

It turns me on to see how my touch affects him, to see him losing control because of what I'm doing. I scoot down and he watches me through slitted eyes as I take him in my mouth. His muscles tighten under my hands and he goes completely still. I get the sense that he's trying to hold himself in check and I find I don't want him controlled. I want to take him past reason and make him lose all sense of time and place the way he did for me.

I relax my throat taking more of him in.

His strangled curse is extremely gratifying and I feel like a sex goddess when his hand tangles in my hair, holding me in place for the thrust of his hips.

Everything about this turns me on: the tormented sounds coming from his throat, the tight grip of his fist in my hair but most of all the look of complete adulation on his face.

He pulls back and then arranges me gently on my stomach. With my ass in the air I feel completely open and exposed.

Every sound is magnified and the crinkle of the condom wrapper as he tears it open makes me jump.

"*Hurry*," I urge him on and then shiver when his hand lands on my ass. He kneads the muscle before squeezing gently.

The anticipation of what he's going to do to me is driving me crazy. I'm so aroused I can feel my moisture dripping down my thighs and at his first thrust, I'm so wet I take him in one smooth stroke.

I'm pushing back to meet him, taking him so deep this way and I know I'll still be feeling it tomorrow. But as I let go and shatter for the second time I realize that's what I want.

I want to feel him tomorrow and every day after that.

———

Sex in the past was always a quick, rushed thing, a little shameful and a lot awkward. It was something I had to do to scratch an itch. I've never wanted to wallow in someone's touch, absorb their every breath and stay skin to skin.

I never knew I could crave someone's touch.

After getting rid of the condom, Luke hasn't let go of me once. Even now, instead of rolling over and falling asleep like most guys, he has me cradled in his arms. He's up on his fore-arms keeping his weight off me, kissing every inch of my face.

The whisper of his lips over my skin is so soft it almost tick-les. It's so sweet, it's like he's just breathing me in because he can't get enough but it's also extremely relaxing. It's the perfect come down after the intensity of making love.

I didn't even know it was possible to feel so much, so fast.

My back aches a little from when I was arching off the bed. *Aches*. I have a sex injury. The thought is so ridiculous that I have to hold back a giggle. Boring Sarah Parker has finally had the kind of wild, crazy sex that leaves you hurting for days afterward.

"Did I hurt you? Be honest," he whispers.

I push back slightly so I can see his eyes. The worry in them absolutely melts me. He's looking me over like he's worried I'll break any minute.

"You didn't do anything I wasn't begging you for."

My breathing gets deeper just thinking about some of the things I said in the heat of the moment. I have no doubt that I was actually begging at some point.

"I'm glad you came with me tonight. Not just because of this, either. Having you there made it so much easier."

He lowers his forehead until it touches mine and we stay like that for a few moments just breathing the same air.

"Were you nervous about being in the wedding?"

I'm curious about how I could have made things easier for him. If anything I expect that my presence stirred up a lot of questions. After all, his family and friends admitted they aren't used to seeing him with anyone.

"No. It's not that."

He hesitates and his eyes search mine. It's usually me with the confessions so my hands instinctively come up to caress his back. I know how hard it can be to bear your soul to someone, unsure of what their reaction might be.

"It's just that my brothers ... well, they've always had some-one. Tank and Finn grew up together and so did Gabe and Zack."

"But you were alone," I finish for him after he pauses. He nods.

Suddenly I understand their strange dynamic better. Luke loves his brothers, I can tell, but there are times when it seems like he's standing back and observing them, unsure of where he fits in.

He's told me before how it was being the biracial kid of a single mother. How he felt like an interloper even among his own family at times. Like me, he's always felt like he's on the outside looking in.

"You're not alone anymore," I promise.

If I hadn't met Luke, I would have never experienced this closeness. Never known that I could be so comfortable with someone and feel so cherished. I'm not even sure what to do now.

Part of me wants to throw my arms around him and never let him leave this bed but I don't want him to think I'm needy or get freaked out. For all I know it wasn't as great for him. Maybe he has mind-blowing sex all the time and this is just another night.

He lowers himself next to me but still doesn't let go. Instead, his arm comes around my waist. With one swift tug, he anchors me to him. Cozied up under his arm, I'm enveloped in his body heat from head to toe.

"Do you need anything, baby?"

Is he joking? What would he do, I wonder, if I said I was ready for round three? I can't even laugh at the idea, I'm too tired. All I can do is muster a satisfied sigh.

"*Mmm*, I'm good. What about you?"

His deep chuckle rumbles against my hair. "I have what I need." His arm tightens around me.

We stay just like that, breathing together. Just when I'm on the verge of sleep, he speaks. His voice in the quiet room startles me.

"You know, you can still call on me when you need me, right? You can tell me anything."

Suddenly I'm wide awake. Now that I've burned off all the champagne, it's so tempting to confess it all. The idea of not having half-truths and outright lies between us would be wonderful but I can't risk it. The only thing I've ever had for sure is Grace and I'll do anything to protect that.

She's the only family I have. What if Luke doesn't understand why I did it? Then I'll lose him *and* Grace.

"I know," I say finally.

That seems to satisfy him because he just squeezes me tighter and dots several sleepy kisses on the back of my neck. I fall asleep wishing I could be satisfied so easily.

---

*L*ater that night, I wake. I'm not used to sleeping in this room so I'm momentarily disoriented. Luke is on the other side of the bed typing on his laptop. At some point he must have gotten up because he's got on a T-shirt and some boxer shorts. His brow is crinkled as he types, like he's troubled. It's surprising how much it bothers me to see him like that. Immediately I want to comfort and help him.

I sit up and all my muscles protest. That's when I remember exactly why I'm in this room. And what we were up doing half the night.

He glances over at me. When he sees how slowly I'm moving, he gives me a sheepish smile. "Sore, huh?"

"Yeah. We were a little enthusiastic earlier."

He puts his laptop on the night table. "I hope I didn't wake you."

"I'm a light sleeper. That's not your fault. I've always had trouble sleeping." You'd think it would be impossible for me to be bashful after the things we did earlier, the places I had my mouth, but somehow I still manage it. I can barely look him in the eye.

"Me too. My mom used to say my mind was too busy." He moves closer and pulls me against him.

I snuggle up to him, burying my face in his shirt and directly into that perfect *Luke* smell.

"Busy. I like that. It makes me feel productive instead of defective. Do you mind if I do some work, too? Or are you ready to go back to sleep now?"

"No, go ahead. I rarely sleep regular hours."

I get out of bed before remembering that I'm completely naked. His eyes roam over me hungrily as I hastily snatch the sheet from the end of the bed and wrap it around me. His eyes follow my movements as I edge out of the room.

My laptop bag is in the living room next to the couch. I grab my laptop and carry it back to bed with me. Luke is absorbed in whatever he's working on so I open my email and start deleting all the junk mail.

Then I see a message from an unfamiliar address. When I look closer, I realize that it's an FBI email address. The subject simply says *status update*.

I freeze, my eyes darting over to Luke. His eyes are still glued to his screen so I open the email.

ETA on project. Please respond.

There's no signature but I don't need one to know who it's from. Agent Walker has been completely quiet over the past week but did I seriously think he was going to give me an unlimited timeframe to get the job done? He was explicit in his instructions. Get him a way into Luke's computer and he would take care of the rest.

In exchange, I would get immunity for all my past indiscretions and he'd ensure that my petition for custody of Grace would go through.

But I should have known that there would be unforeseen repercussions of this Faustian bargain. I never thought it would be easy to betray a friend but Agent Walker had assured me that Luke wasn't their target. They just wanted to get intel on his father.

It hadn't seemed like such a bad exchange at the time. After all, I knew that Luke didn't even *know* his father.

But after meeting his brothers and their wives and girlfriends, it doesn't seem like such a simple exchange. What if something they find out has repercussions for one of his brothers? I have no way of knowing if something on his computer could implicate one of them. Everything that seemed so crystal clear a week ago is suddenly complicated as hell.

I delete the email and then clear my trash. I'm really good at putting my head in the sand and for once I don't berate myself for it. This night with Luke has been one of the best in my life and I don't want to let anything intrude on that. Tomorrow is soon enough to face the consequences of my actions.

Luke closes his laptop and puts it back on his nightstand.

I look up and force a smile. "Are you ready to sleep? I'm done." I close my computer too and set it gently on the floor.

When I turn back around, I notice my sheet is slipping. I grab at it but it keeps moving downward. That's when I realize it's not slipping.

Luke is pulling it off.

He yanks harder and the sheet slides off completely. My nipples pebble in the cool air. Desire returns so swiftly I'm left light-headed. His head descends and goosebumps spread everywhere his lips touch.

As he kisses his way up my leg, I finally gather my voice enough to ask, "Aren't we going to sleep now?"

He looks up from the cradle of my thighs. "I'll sleep when I'm dead."

Chapter Fifteen

Luke

The next morning I wake early. Seven is curled up next to me and somehow seeing her there seems ... right. Like it's where she should have always been. I climb out of bed carefully and then tuck the blanket back around her. She sighs in her sleep and burrows deeper into the warmth. I kiss her forehead and then close the door to the room as I step out into the hall.

While the coffee is brewing, I check my email. I grin when I see that my father's assistant is apparently an insomniac, too. She read the email I sent sometime last night. Five minutes later, she clicked the link and entered her password.

"Just like riding a bike," I whisper.

I use the passcode she's provided to log on to Max's company server using her first initial and last name. It's a gamble. I'm assuming she's using the same password for her company access that she uses at the bank but so many people do that it's a pretty safe bet. Sure enough, it works and I now have access to her email, calendar, and all her files. She's pretty organized which makes it easier to know what to bypass. She even has a folder labeled *Mr. Marshall*.

I sip my coffee as I take a stroll through her system. It doesn't take long before I come across a Word document labeled *Just in Case* that has all the passwords for Max's accounts listed out. I shake my head. This is almost too easy.

That's when I start reading his email.

Most of it is boring and I can tell his assistant writes most of these messages. There are a lot of emails asking for him to fund certain business ventures or about social events he's declined to attend. It's hard to determine what my father actually does for a living but from his correspondence it appears he mainly tells other people what to do.

Then I notice an email marked for deletion. Even though it's not in the Inbox anymore, it hasn't been cleared from his Trash yet. The sender is listed as Cabhan Marshall.

It's an innocuous looking message at first glance, something about the sale of a pair of old golf clubs. But the fact that there are no other messages from this sender in his Inbox at all makes me curious. If the message is so innocent, why delete it?

And the idea of billionaire industrialist Max Marshall buying used *anything* is just ridiculous.

I start combing through his messages more carefully and notice a few others that seem to be about random things. If it's some kind of code then I can't decipher it but maybe the FBI can. My father even has a Facebook account which I log in to just to see if he's ever used it.

I find Cabhan Marshall in his friends list and copy some of his profile pictures. I'm able to find names corresponding to the senders of a few other weird emails so I grab pictures for them, too.

When I first found out that my father wanted back into my life, of course I started digging around for information. I found out about his ties to the Irish Mafia even before he told us himself. His story about breaking free from the secretive fringe group Le Fírinne' was at times unbelievable and other times heartbreaking.

For the first time since he came back into our lives, my resolve to have nothing to do with him wavered. All things considered, my father appeared to be a man born into bad circumstances who did everything he could to get out.

The day he told us his story, after Gabe was stabbed by one of Max's nephews who works for the family, Max seemed to understand why I stayed away. He told us himself that leaving us behind was the best thing he could do for us.

He wanted us to have the chance to grow up independent of the criminal element he could never escape.

Once I realized the authorities were hot on his trail, I tried to warn my brothers to stay away from him, too. Not that it did any good.

But I knew that the only thing protecting me was my determination to stay as far away from Max Marshall as possible. Any contact could make me seem complicit in whatever shady dealings Max still has in the works and even if I had no sense of self-preservation, I wouldn't want that element anywhere near my mom.

My goal is to grab anything and everything that might have some relevance. I'll comb through it later and delete anything I think could implicate Max directly but it's probably going to be hard to keep him out of this completely. Based on what Max told us himself, he played an integral role in Le Fírinne' since his youth.

I transfer everything to my own server Gabe then make a few changes to Max's calendar. It's going to take some time to go through everything. Just thinking about it makes me tired but it's necessary.

I need all the ammunition I can get if I'm going to negotiate with the FBI. Especially since I don't know what they have on Seven in the first place.

There's a chance I can't bargain my way out of this but I'll be damned if I don't try.

———

I arrive at the restaurant in Norfolk for my meeting with Max a few days later deliberately early. I want to be here when my father walks in but I also wanted to get out of the house.

Things have been tense over the last few days. Seven has been distant and nothing I've done has coaxed it out of her. The only time things feel right is at night when she comes to my bed.

Our connection there is just as hot as ever.

I give my name at the door as Mr. Holden Williams, which of course matches the reservation I made, and am seated immediately.

After ten minutes, the hostess appears with Max trailing slowly behind her. I'm always surprised by how old and frail he seems. His suit hangs off his frame like he's lost a bit of weight recently and the wisps of white hair on his head don't appear to have been combed recently. Or ever.

They stop next to the table and I stand. Max doesn't look surprised to see me at all. Neither of us speaks.

"Is there anything else you require, sir?" She looks between us in confusion, probably wondering why we're not greeting each other.

"No, that'll be all." Max dismisses her with an impatient flick of the wrist.

He sits carefully, using his cane to leverage himself down. I wait, unsure whether he needs me to help him. I'm shocked at the instinct to do so. For years, I've carried nothing but anger for my father but now that he's here in front of me, I'm not mad anymore. I'm just tired.

Once he's seated, he lets out a long sigh. "Getting old is hell."

"You don't seem that surprised to see me."

He smiles at the blunt statement. "I'm old but my mind is still just as sharp as a tack. Holden and I only meet every six months or so and he always calls me first. When Carol told me I was scheduled to meet with him today, I knew something was off. My boys checked it out first."

He looks over his shoulder and that's when I notice the big guys sitting a few tables away.

"I figured you must have your reasons for needing to see me. Even if the method was a little unorthodox."

"I do. I'm afraid this isn't a social visit. I'm here to warn you. The FBI is circling and they're trying to use me to get to you."

His eyes meet mine. "I'm sorry they're bothering you. They've been hovering in the wings for years, just waiting for me to step out of line. I get the feeling they're disappointed every year that passes when I stay on the straight and narrow. Makes me long for the days when I could occasionally blow some shit up just to keep things interesting."

Despite everything, I can't help but laugh at that. I wouldn't say I see myself in him but the next time I wonder where I inherited my penchant for giving zero fucks, I'll remember this conversation.

"You're a crazy old bird, you know that?"

"I'll take that as a compliment. I always thought of myself as a phoenix. A fighter that rises from the ashes of its own demise."

The waiter appears and we both order the special. He leaves, sensing that neither of us cares about food. As soon as he's gone, I lean across the table.

"Look, the FBI has been trying to hack me for years. But now they're threatening someone I love. I have to do something."

His hand shakes as he reaches for his water glass. "What are you trying to tell me, Luke?"

When I planned this meeting, I never imagined that I'd feel so guilty. For years this man has represented nothing but pain in my life. But now that he's here in front of me, it's not so easy to tell him that I'm throwing him under the bus.

"I hacked into your computer system. You should tell your assistant never to click on links in emails. And to stop using the same password for everything."

He blinks several times and then a booming laugh rings out. "I'll do that. You've got balls, kid. That's for sure."

"This isn't a joke. I have to give the FBI something. If I'm going to negotiate, I have to offer something they want. What they want is information about *you*."

"Don't worry about me. No matter what happens, the world will keep on spinning. It always does."

The fact that he's trying to reassure me makes it all the worse. He's worried about my conscience while I'm burning his world to the ground.

"I'm going to do my best to scrub the information. Pull out anything that can implicate you directly but chances are that I'll miss something. Consider this a friendly warning to be on your guard."

He inclines his head in acknowledgment. "I understand. You're just doing what you have to do. A man has to protect those he loves, a lesson I learned too late. Although I suppose if I hadn't been so foolish once you wouldn't be here. And I wouldn't choose that for anything."

He observes me quietly for a moment. There's no denying that the way he's looking at me is ... fond. I was expecting him to be annoyed or even angry that I've refused to meet with him before. The last thing I was expecting was to show up and realize that he loves me.

"I just wanted to warn you ahead of time. I feel like I owe you that much."

"You don't owe me anything. But I thank you for it all the same." He places his napkin down on the table and grabs his cane.

"Wait, where are you going?"

He blinks in surprise. "You brought me here to warn me. Which I appreciate. Now I'll let you get back to that pretty little thing at your apartment."

I don't even bother asking how he knows about Seven. He seems to have eyes everywhere. I guess that's a side effect of constantly worrying about someone stabbing you in the back.

"Well, don't go yet."

My mom has always said that kindness costs nothing but is worth everything. Considering things are probably going to get pretty dicey after this, would it really hurt for me to spend a little time with him? I look around and in that moment I make a decision.

"Stay. We're already here. We might as well have lunch."

He smiles tremulously and then rests his cane against the table. "Having lunch with my son. I'd like that very much."

———

By the time I get home a few hours later, I'm running on fumes. Talking to Max was surprisingly easy and had the unwelcome side effect of making me second-guess my decision.

I've never missed having a father. How can you miss something you've never had? But I did wonder what it would be like. I watched other kids with their fathers at baseball games and at the park. It's way too late for Max and I to ever bond that way but tonight I saw that it's not necessarily too late for me to know him.

He's smart and has an unexpectedly sharp sense of humor. He has all the brashness of Tank and a sense of charm that reminds me of Gabe. I can easily see bits and pieces of all of us in him and it makes me wonder what I've done.

Max was able to provide some details that will help me scrub the information I pulled. He told me who was friend and who was foe. But even with that information, I still have a sick sense of foreboding about this whole thing.

What if he really does end up going to prison because of me? I was so sure I wouldn't care and one meal changed everything.

I shake off my sense of guilt as I open the door. The living room is empty but Seven's shoes are in the middle of the floor and her favorite coffee mug is on the table. My earlier sense of unease vanishes instantly. I don't owe anything to Max just because we're related. I have an obligation only to myself and to those I care about. And more and more, I'm starting to consider Seven "mine." Mine to protect. Mine to cherish.

Mine to love.

Her things look right in my place. *She* looks right in my place. It's where she belongs and I'm going to fix things for her. If I give the FBI information they want, they'll leave Seven alone.

I'll protect her with the last breath in my body.

Things are quiet but then I hear soft singing coming from the bedroom. Seven's probably working with headphones on again.

I pull out the laptop I bought on the way home. It doesn't take long to configure and then pull the information from my server. I glance at my phone, occasionally referencing the list of names Max gave me as I decide what to include. Finally I have a reasonable cache of information that should keep the FBI appeased. Hopefully.

I walk back to the bathroom, leaving the laptop open on the counter. If Seven downloads whatever is on that flash drive, the FBI will get exactly what I want them to see. It'll kill me if she does it but even if she betrays me, she'll be protected.

I'll keep her safe even if she doesn't want me to. My heart won't allow me to do any less.

Chapter Sixteen

Seven

This morning, I was only half awake when Luke kissed me goodbye. I heard something about an appointment but I was asleep again before he left the room. By the time I wake again it's almost lunchtime.

It's probably a good thing that Luke isn't here to witness my painfully awkward walk to the bathroom. I've never thought of myself as being in bad shape but we definitely gave my muscles a much needed workout again last night. I'm stiff and sore all over, even after I stand under the hot spray of the shower for a solid ten minutes.

Amidst the warmth and steam I acknowledge that I'm using sex to distract me from the rapidly looming deadline. Agent

Walker hasn't emailed me again yet but it's coming. It's only a matter of time. Luke has definitely sensed that something is wrong but he doesn't seem to want to delve too deeply either.

I think we're both afraid of upsetting this delicate equilibrium we've reached.

Maybe if I get some work done I'll be in a better frame of mind to come up with a plan. I get out and towel off, then dress in jeans and a T-shirt before sitting down behind my computer. After a while, I get up and put on my headphones. I'm not used to being in the apartment alone and the quiet seems so loud. Luke didn't say what his appointment was about but he's been gone for a long time.

Insecurity threatens and I wonder if he's seeking space from the recent tension between us. Can I really blame him if he is? It's been a strain on me, too. My feelings for him have me all turned around.

An hour into working on my newest game, I'm immersed in my music when I hear a loud sound. I pull my headphones off and stretch. "Luke?"

There's no answer.

I save my progress and then close my laptop. When I open the bedroom door, I hear the shower running in the bathroom across the hall. I walk into the kitchen and then stop.

Luke's laptop is on the counter. And he's left it logged in.

This is the exact opportunity I've been waiting for. His guard is down and he thinks I'm asleep. This could all be over and I could be on the train home to New York first thing in the morning. I'd finally have everything I've always wanted most, Grace safe and sound with me. We'd be a family.

My laptop bag is next to the couch. I retrieve the flash drive from the side pocket and then carry it back over to the counter. Luke was looking at Facebook. The page is still open on the screen. His profile picture stares back at me. I drop the flash drive on the table and run my hands over my face.

I can't do it.

When I started this, I thought it would be so simple. Wipe my legal slate clean and get the thing I want most in the world, custody of Grace. But that's not the only thing I care about now. I want something for myself, too.

Luke. I want Luke.

The first sob takes me off guard, so much so that it actually startles me. I clap a hand over my mouth to hold it in and it feels like I'm holding back more than just the sound. I'm holding myself together by a string.

Then suddenly, I'm not holding myself together at all. Luke is.

He wraps his arms around me from behind and buries his face in my neck. "I knew you wouldn't do it. I knew it."

"Oh god." I turn in his arms and hold on to his shirt for dear life. He hooks his elbows under my knees and lifts me, carrying me back to the bedroom. I cling to him, feeling like he's the only thing real and true in the world. He sits on the bed, holding me securely in his arms.

No talking. No questions. Just us.

By the time the tears have run their course, I'm limp and wrung out like a dishrag. That's about how I feel, anyway.

Finally I lift my head. "How did you know?"

He brushes my hair off my face. "I figured it out a while back. You were being so weird. Hot and then cold. Happy and then sad. I could tell you were conflicted about something. All I had to do was think back to how we met. All roads lead to the FBI."

"I *was* conflicted. *Tortured.*"

"You think I don't know that?" He chuckles and the sound makes me feel less panicked. I'm not sure how he can be so calm when I feel like I'm in the middle of a tempest. "What did they threaten you with?"

I sigh. "I've done some things I'm not proud of. For a while I took any job that paid well. Legal or not. They said all would be forgiven."

"And?" He raises his eyebrows. "What else? I know you, Sev. You wouldn't have even been tempted if they just threatened to arrest you. They have to be holding something big over your head for you to have even considered it."

Is it any wonder I can't resist him? The man doesn't miss a thing and he knows me better than anyone.

"Grace. They said my petition for custody of Grace won't go through if I don't help them. They promised that they weren't after you. Just information you might have on your father."

"I should have known," he says.

He leans back until he's flat on the bed, pulling me down with him. I listen to his breathing, the steady rhythm soothing after that wrenching crying jag. Finally my heart rate feels normal again.

"I'm so sorry, Luke." The words seem so inadequate but they're all I have to offer. And I mean them with every part of my soul.

"So am I, baby."

Surprised, I sit up. "What are *you* sorry for?"

"For not ending this sooner. I could see what it was doing to you, how it was tearing you apart. I should have told you that I knew. That's what I'm sorry for. Letting you suffer needlessly."

I shake my head. "I'm the one who lied. You've done nothing but listen to me. Take care of me. And this whole time I was plotting to hurt you."

"Like that day in the park? Why didn't you do it then?" he challenges.

"Because .... Well, I don't know."

He guffaws. "You had plenty of time to do it when I was on the phone that day. Or any one of these days when I was asleep. You've seen me type my password so many times you could probably figure it out with a few tries."

I can see what he's getting at but I'm not ready to let myself off the hook so easily. This was something I did with my eyes wide open and it was wrong. No amount of sugarcoating can change that.

"I'm a coward, apparently. I was scared of getting caught."

"You didn't want to. It's as simple as that." He kisses me on the nose.

All my resolve melts like butter. God, he's so sweet and always in my corner. He has my back even when I don't deserve it. Who could stay strong when faced with an opponent this cute?

"No, I didn't want to. I never want to hurt you, Luke. I just want ... to love you."

His eyes glow and he flips us over so he's on top. My legs fall open naturally to accept him in the cradle of my thighs. He settles against me and I can't hold back a little moan as he grinds against me. The sound is swallowed up between us when he kisses me.

"Say it again," he mumbles against my lips.

"I love you, Luke."

"I love you, too." He kisses me deeper, entwining our fingers together over our heads. My hand flexes in his as he turns me on deftly with just a few flicks of his tongue.

"Mmm, now that we've gotten that established we have to figure out what we're going to do."

I wrap my arms around him, pulling him closer. It doesn't seem real that he shares my feelings. I want to hang on and never let go.

"What can we do? Eventually Agent Walker is going to realize I'm deleting his emails and then I'm sure I'll be arrested. For real this time. I don't even know what the FBI has on me."

"Probably not much but I'm going to give them something to keep them off your back just in case. Where's that flash drive?"

He pushes up off the bed and extends his hand to help me up. Reluctantly, I take it and then follow him up front to the living room. His laptop is still on the counter. The flash drive is right next to it.

"Whatever they told you to do to my computer, do it."

I spin around. "What? Luke, no way! I'm not giving them access to your system."

He covers my mouth with his until my protests turn into soft moans.

"Baby, that's not my computer." He gestures to the laptop on the counter. "It's the same make and model but it's not the one I usually use. See?"

Upon closer inspection I can tell that this computer is newer than the one I've seen him working on.

"So you left this out here to test me?"

"I wouldn't say that. I just made sure that no matter which choice you made, I could live with the consequences. But I knew all along you'd never go through with it."

"You did?"

"Of course." He wraps his arms around me from behind. "You're always saving me, remember? It's not in your nature to hurt someone you care about it. No matter what. But that's not the only reason this laptop is here. It's not just a decoy. It's a peace offering."

I raise an eyebrow. "What does that mean?"

He kisses me soundly on the neck and then grabs the flash drive. "It has all the information about my father's shady associates that I could find. This should keep Agent Walker happy without giving him anything I don't want him to see."

"Do you really think this will work?"

"I can only hope so. But I guess there's only one way to find out. Do it."

He watches as I put the flash drive in the USB port. Once it shows up on screen, I double-click the file on it to open it.

"There. I guess there's no going back now. I hope this works."

He lifts me in his arms. "I'm sure it will. In the meantime there's a few things we need to discuss."

"Oh? Things like what?" My smile grows when his hands dip under the hem of my T-shirt.

"Well, I can't let this go without some sort of punishment. I'm sure you understand."

I giggle all the way back to the bedroom.

———

Luke's brand of punishment is more like pleasure. Lots and lots of pleasure. We float together on a cloud of bliss fueled only by our desire for each other. By the time we come up for air, it's almost midnight.

"We should probably stop for food and water at some point," Luke mentions between suctioning kisses to my spine.

I sigh at each tender touch, my skin tingling all over from being rubbed, teased and scratched. The more he touches me, the more I seem to want him. It's an insatiable desire he's stoked in me, like a wild animal that's never quite fed.

I find I like being wild with him.

"Food is probably a good idea." But I'm too lazy and satisfied to move. It's so tempting to stay here in this bed and ignore the outside world forever. But despite the fact that everything is out in the open now, there's still the very real threat of us being torn apart.

My mind runs through every worst case scenario, from Agent Walker arresting me despite Luke's peace offering, to him deliberately messing with Grace's custody situation to punish me. My little bubble of happiness leaks away and I shiver under the reality of all the bad possibilities still out there on the horizon.

"You just tensed up. What's going on in there?" Luke kisses the side of my head and then pulls me back into his embrace. It's my favorite place to be, wrapped up in his arms and surrounded by his love.

"Just thinking about everything. About what happens if this doesn't work."

He sighs. I turn over to face him. "Thank you again for what you did. I haven't forgotten that I'm not the only one with a lot at stake here."

"It's all going to be fine. If this doesn't work, something else will. We can always figure out a solution as long as we do it together. No more secrets."

That's a promise I can get behind. It killed me to hide things from him before and that's not a mistake I'll ever repeat. "I promise to always tell you the truth. Even if it's that your feet are *cold*."

He cracks up and then presses the soles of his feet harder against my shins. I howl as the ice cold skin makes contact.

"*Holy shit.* You'll pay for that!"

We roll around and around on top of the covers until I manage to straddle him. He's still laughing when I plant my hands on his chest pushing him down. Of course, he could easily overpower me if he wanted to but he allows me to hold him down.

"I surrender."

His hips flex, pressing his cock against me. He enjoys letting me take the reins for sure. But I can tell he's just as exhausted as I am. Neither of us has the energy to deliver on any erotic threats right now so I snuggle against his chest, listening to his heartbeat as it thumps beneath my cheek.

Something occurs to me as I'm drifting toward sleep.

"Luke?"

"Hmm?"

"I know you said you only put stuff you want them to see on that computer but what happens if that stuff leads them to other things? Things that get your father in trouble?"

His muscles tighten beneath my chest and by the sudden tension in his body, I know this isn't the first time he's considered this scenario.

"Oh Luke. I never meant for you to have to choose between me and your family. I would never want you to do that." That's basically what Agent Walker was trying to force me to do, choose between my sister and my best friend. I would never put him in that position.

He sits up, taking me with him until we're chest to chest. Forehead to forehead. His hands gather up the long waves of my hair and he uses the long tail to hold me still.

"Seven, listen closely. It wasn't even a choice. *You* are my family. And I will do whatever I have to do to keep you safe."

I can feel the truth behind what he's saying with every word. When he told me he loves me, he really meant it.

I guess love isn't only for the lucky few after all.

Chapter Seventeen

Luke

Over the next few weeks, things are quiet. Seven and I are both on pins and needles waiting for something, *anything*, to happen. But Agent Walker doesn't contact her again and though we're watching the news carefully for any mention of arrests, there's nothing.

It's too soon to declare victory but as we approach a month without calamity, I start breathing a little easier. We called their bluff and nothing bad happened. I'm not sure who is looking out for us upstairs but it appears that Seven's been granted a *get out of jail free* card.

And so has my father, apparently.

Slowly the knot of uncertainty that's been lodged in my

stomach loosens and I start to believe that things are going to work out okay.

Then I open the door on a Monday morning to see my mom with tears in her eyes. And I know instantly that something is *very* wrong.

"Mom? What's going on?"

I move back so she can come in the apartment. Seven is sitting at the kitchen counter drinking her coffee. Her eyes widen when she sees my mom and she tugs the hem of the shirt she's wearing lower over her bare thighs.

"Anita! I didn't know you were coming over this morning. I'll just go change." She abandons her coffee on the counter and edges out of the room, giving me a mortified glance before her face disappears around the corner.

"Is everything okay, Mom? Is Grandpop in the hospital again?"

She wrings her hands, her keychain jingling with the nervous movement. When I see the look on her face, the knot in my stomach is back.

"Oh, sweetheart. You haven't been online today at all, have you?"

I shake my head mutely. She watches helplessly as I stroke the mouse pad on Seven's laptop to wake it up. There's always a laptop accessible in our place. And now that we're together, we know all of each other's passwords. Neither of us has anything to hide.

Her homepage is a search engine so I pull up the MSN homepage. The headline stares back at me.

Billionaire mogul Max Marshall dies in FBI raid.

When I was a little boy and something scared me, my mom used to make up a story about it. Like if I was scared of a bug, she'd tell me a story about the bug walking home after a long day to see his family. Or about how the monster under my bed was really a misunderstood creature who liked the dark instead of the sunlight.

For the first time in a long time, I wish that she could spin a story for me to make it all better. Tell me that my father is on a long vacation or that he's the captain of a pirate ship and out to sea. But as I stare at the black and white letters on the screen, I know there's no way to spin this story that can make it better.

Nothing can change the sick certainty that my actions are directly responsible for my father's death.

"I called you several times this morning. Then when you didn't pick up I came straight here."

Her voice recedes in the background as I walk over to the window overlooking the parking lot. It's a beautiful day, the contrast of the bright sun to the devastation going on inside my head almost ironic. I recognize a few of my neighbors walking to their cars, holding coffee mugs and purses.

It's all so normal.

What was it Max said to me? No matter what happens, the world just keeps right on spinning. Something like that. It suddenly seems vital that I remember his exact words, the last wisdom he shared with me. We had so little time together and what we had, I didn't appreciate.

Now it's too late.

A while later I come back to myself and realize that I've been standing at the window for a long time. My mom and Seven whisper behind me and I can feel their concern in the air. It wraps around me, choking me.

I'm not sure that I can do this right now. Say the right things and appear fine. Not now.

"I'm going out."

Seven rushes around the kitchen counter. She's changed clothes into one of the loose sundresses she loves so much. I love them on her, too. This one is a soft yellow. She looks like a ray of sunshine peeking through the clouds.

I don't deserve sunshine and rainbows.

"Okay, I'll come with you—"

"No. I need to go ... I need to be alone right now."

Hurt flashes across her face but she smiles, putting on a brave face. Her hand tugs at the ends of her hair. The sight of the nervous gesture only underlines my determination that I'm not good company for her right now. I love her too much to let my darkness take her, too.

"Okay, whatever you need."

My mom watches as I grab my keys from the counter and then pull on a hat. "I'll walk you outside. I need to get to the bakery. Rory can only handle things until ten."

Seven hugs her. "Thank you for coming over, Anita."

"Call me later and let me know how he's doing." My mom's whisper carries across the room.

"I will. I'll let you know if he needs anything." Seven glances over at me and her eyelashes flutter when she realizes I'm listening.

My mom holds out her hand to me just like she used to when I was little. I take it, holding on to her all the way downstairs and until we're standing next to her car.

"Luke, I know this is terrible. An awful tragedy. I just want you to know that you can talk to me if you need to. Or talk to Seven. But whatever you do, don't hold it all inside."

She leans up and kisses me on the cheek. I watch until her car pulls out of the parking lot. My phone beeps. It's a message from Tank.

Meet us at Gabe's place.

At least now I have a destination. I get in the car and drive. By the time I pull into Gabe's driveway, I realize I don't remember anything of the ride over. The front door of the house opens before I even get out of the car and I recognize Tank's tall frame.

When I cross the threshold, his hand lands on my shoulder and the tension inside only twists tighter.

Gabe, Zack and Finn are already inside. They all look like hell. None of us seems to know what to say so we just sit around in stunned silence. Finally Tank speaks.

"I pulled some strings to find out what happened. The official story is that Max was taken into FBI custody and died while he was being brought in. His heart couldn't take the stress of being arrested."

He runs a hand through his hair in frustration. "That's all I could find out so far."

Finn puts an arm around his shoulder. "He was in his seventies, right? Why the hell would they take in an old man that way? There are ways to take someone in without terrorizing them."

Zack looks up. "Maybe I shouldn't have called him back to the States. He came back to meet with me and then he just stayed, I guess. If I hadn't done that, he'd probably be hiding out on a beach somewhere."

Gabe nudges him. "Don't think like that. There's no way you could have known what would happen. Besides, when does Max ever stick around somewhere just for the hell of it? He probably was here for another reason and it had nothing to do with us."

"Yeah, I guess." Zack doesn't look convinced but he doesn't offer anything else.

I look at my brothers. Tank and Finn stand on one side, Gabe and Zack on the other. They instinctively move toward the sibling they grew up with.

And as usual, I'm alone.

I open my mouth to tell them the part they don't know. That he was only arrested because I handed him over on a silver platter. That I warned him but it was too little, too late. That I killed our father.

But somehow the words don't come.

My mom was right. It is a terrible thing. And it's all my fault.

———

Three days later, I stand in front of the mirror in my bedroom putting on a tie for the second time this year. Dressing up isn't something I usually do. *Weddings and funerals*, I think.

Is it any wonder most men hate wearing suits? For the blue-collar among us they represent only the highs and lows of the human experience. Usually the lows because honestly, how often does life hand out lemonade?

I'm going to burn this suit after today.

Seven appears in the doorway. Her dark hair is pulled back into a severe braid and her skin seems so pale against her black dress. It's been a rough couple of days and the stress shows in her face. It only underscores my guilt to see how my emotional absence has taken a toll on her.

I've tried not to pull away, worried that she'd interpret my distance as blame. But I can tell that she's in her own personal hell, knowing that the bargain we made to save her future condemned my father to death.

"The car is here."

I pull her into my arms and kiss her on the forehead. She places a cool hand on my cheek, and then follows me outside and into the limo waiting at the curb. I have no idea who arranged this, no idea who arranged any of this since the last few days have been such a blur. I assume my father's staff has handled the funeral arrangements or maybe some relative I'm unaware of.

The idea of other Marshall relatives coming out of the woodwork at this point is so absurd that I have the insane urge to start laughing. If I have any other siblings out there, they'd do best to stay away from me. If Max had done that he might still be alive.

The limo glides to a stop in front of West Haven's only funeral home.

"I'm surprised Max wanted to be buried here instead of at home."

"Actually, this is just the memorial service. His body is being flown back to Ireland to be buried in the family plot tomorrow."

Seven squeezes my hand and I squeeze back, hoping that I can convey how grateful I am that she's here. If she wasn't holding me together I think I would have been shredded by guilt by now and I'd just blow away in a million little pieces.

We file into the funeral home and Tank greets us at the door. My head is a blur as I shake hands with so many people, none of whom I will remember later. We follow Gabe and Sasha up front and sit in the front row. Zack and Josie are already there. Sitting in the row behind us, I see Claire, Tank and Finn's mom.

Carol, the assistant I hacked all those weeks ago, taps on the microphone set up in front of the casket.

"Hello. My name is Carol Ryan." She glances down at the little scrap of paper in her hand. "I first met Max Marshall when I was a twenty-two-year-old waitress at an Irish pub in Boston. My parents had kicked me out and I was on my own for the first time. Max gave me a job. He took care of me then and I've been taking care of him ever since. He was more than just an employer. He was a friend."

She stops to collect herself. After a few deep breaths, she motions behind her at the closed casket. "Max wasn't one for making a fuss so he left explicit instructions that there aren't to be any tears. Just reflections on a life well lived."

She sits and someone else I don't recognize gets up and reads a poem. Then a trio sings a sad lament in Gaelic that brings a lump to my throat even if I don't understand a word of it. When the last mournful note trails off, people stand and start leaving.

I stand, content to just follow the flow of traffic when Tank leans over his seat and tugs my arm.

"Luke, come on. Max's lawyer has something for us."

"I'll wait for you here." Seven kisses me on the cheek and then goes to stand with Sasha, Josie and Emma.

Tank leads us into a room off the back. An older man meets us at the door and motions for us to come inside. He seems very somber and I wonder if it's just because of the occasion or if he and Max were actually friends. I've never met this particular lawyer before but that's not surprising. I'm pretty sure Max has always employed a team of them for his many interests.

He motions for us to sit in the chairs in front of the desk. There isn't enough room so Tank and I lean against the wall near the door.

"Thank you for coming. I'm Harold Levitt. Mr. Marshall left explicit instructions for how he wanted his will to be read. So I'll just proceed."

Finn leans forward. "He told us he distributed his estate early. I assumed that we'd already received our inheritance."

Mr. Levitt places a pair of wire frames on his face. "He distributed a portion of his estate earlier this year, that's true.

However, he has bequeathed an additional sum to each of you."

He clears his throat and begins to read.

I, Maxwell Marshall, direct my executors to pay all estate and inheritance taxes. I give all my tangible personal property to my sons, Tanner, Finnigan, Gabriel, Zachary and Lucas subject to the following conditions ...

It all sounds like a lot of legalese to me but halfway through Tank starts chuckling. Gabe follows suit and then Zack. Finn just smiles with a hand over his mouth.

"Why are you all laughing?" I ask, shocked that they would be this disrespectful while our father's will is being read.

Mr. Levitt doesn't seem at all concerned and in fact when he lowers the paper he's been reading from, I see he's smiling as well.

Tank looks over at me. "Even in death, Max can't resist having the last laugh. He's put conditions on us receiving the remainder of his money. Just like last time. The cranky old bastard wants us all to get married and have kids before we inherit the rest."

Finn shakes his head. "I bet he had a grand time coming up with this idea. It's almost like he's still here."

Mr. Levitt puts down the document he's been reading from. "This is the part where I've been instructed to stop reading *that boring shit*, as Max called it and read his personal missive to you."

He picks up a white envelope and pulls out a single sheet of paper. It's a distinctive shade of blue.

My sons.

If you're hearing this, I'm finally gone. I hope you got a bit of a laugh out of my last will and testament. Had to throw a few curveballs in there just to shake things up. I meant what I told Carol about no tears. This isn't a time for sadness but for joy. Knowing all of you was the culmination of a lifelong dream. You are all the embodiment of the man I could never be.

Until the next lifetime,

Max

Mr. Levitt places the letter carefully back in the envelope. Then he leans down and pulls out a bottle of Jameson.

"Your father requested that we share a drink in his honor. His favorite Irish whiskey for his favorite Irish boys. His words."

He pulls out five glasses and pours a little in each. Tank hands one back to me and I stare at the amber liquid, Max's last words to us rolling around in my head.

We all take a sip and then Tank starts laughing again.

"Only Max could turn a funeral into a pub crawl."

They all laugh again but I can't summon any levity. I'm burdened not just by the loss but by my part in it. Looking back I'm not sure that I would do anything differently. I had a hand to play and I played it. Max himself seemed to understand why I was doing it. He called it *doing what I had to do*. But none of it matters now, does it?

The end result is the same. He's still gone.

I walk out, their laughter echoing behind me. I walk past the girls still sitting in the front row before the altar and past the people congregating in the lobby. Maybe if I walk far enough I can forget that *doing what I had to do* came at a very high price.

One I'm not yet sure how to live with.

Seven

I trot out of the funeral home and look frantically left and right. When Sasha told me she saw Luke walk past, I assumed he was going to the bathroom or just out front to get some air. Not that he wouldn't be coming back.

But it's been an hour and there's no sign of him.

"We drove around the block and didn't see him. Did you try to track his cell phone?"

I nod. That was the first thing I tried. I'm too embarrassed to admit that he's deliberately turned his GPS off. He doesn't want to be found. But that doesn't mean that I can just give up. Tank said that he was upset after hearing his father's last letter.

Even if he doesn't think he wants company right now, he needs it. No one should be alone while they're hurting. I know all too well how that feels.

Another ten minutes goes by and then I see something at the end of the street. "Is that him?"

Tank has been leaning against his car talking on his phone but stands at my shout. He shades his eyes with his hand. He nods at me and then tells whoever is on the other end of the phone, "We found him. I'll call you back."

Luke is walking on the sidewalk, his head down so he hasn't noticed us yet. By the time he gets closer I can see that he looks all disheveled. The legs of his pants are dusty like he's been walking for a long time.

"You're all dirty."

He looks down at his shoes. "Yes. I am."

When he doesn't say anything else, I look over at Tank. He takes the hint.

"Where've you been, bro?"

Luke shrugs. "Walking."

"We were, uh, getting a little worried about you."

"I had to get out of there."

Tank glances over at me. "I'm going to drive you guys home but if you need anything later, don't hesitate to call."

I know that last bit is meant for me. He made sure that I had all of their phone numbers earlier, something I'm grateful for now. The way Luke is responding is really scary. He's answering our questions but the dispassionate way he's speaking sounds like a robot. Like he doesn't really care about anything.

"Come on baby." I'm so grateful that Tank drove since the limo that brought us here is long gone. I climb in the back with Luke, happy when he puts his arm around me instead of pulling away.

Tank waves after he drops us off and Luke follows me into the apartment. He stands there, like he's not sure what he's supposed to do now. I take his hand and lead him back to the bedroom. He allows me to push his suit jacket off his shoulders. I fold it carefully and rest it on the back of his desk chair. Then I unbuckle his belt and pull his shirt out.

I glance up at him. There's something so sad about the way he's allowing me to tend to him. He seems to want someone else to take the lead. I finish stripping him out of his clothes until he's nude then I pull my dress over my head.

His eyes heat and he watches as my bra hits the floor next. Then he grabs me and his lips are moving roughly over mine, almost bruising in their intensity.

"Need you, Sev. Need you so much." He buries his face against my shoulder, holding me so tight I can barely breathe.

Maybe this is what he needs, a reaffirmation of life after all the harsh emotions of the last few days. I kiss him fiercely, hoping he can feel how much I love him. How much I miss him.

It's been so hard to feel him pulling away from me. That first day he couldn't even look at me and I know it's because it made him think about what he had to do. It scares me that I might lose him now after everything we've gone through. I feel so selfish thinking about myself when he's just lost his father but I'd be lying if I pretended I wasn't worried.

I'm terrified that he'll always look at me and see death and pain and loss.

He walks us backward until we end up on the bed, falling in a tangle of arms and legs. He takes my nipple between his lips and then his hand is pulling my thong off. Leveraging above me he thrusts so deep, until I'm stretched almost to the point of pain.

"Yes. That's what I need." His head falls back on his shoulders and I look up at him, glorying in the sight of him in the throes of pleasure. When his eyes fall to mine, he looks tormented.

"Tell me you're mine."

"I'm yours. I'm only yours, Luke."

My whispered promise doesn't seem to satisfy him. He slides deep and grinds against me until I cry out.

"Tell me you'll never leave me."

It's a struggle to open my eyes when he's circling his hips that way. I shudder underneath him but manage to moan, "I'll never leave you, baby."

His agonized groan sends a skitter of sensation down my spine and I arch against him, the taut tips of my breasts brushing his chest.

"Do that again. Clench around me."

I deliberately tighten my internal muscles.

"Fuck."

That sets him off and I lift my hips, trying to match his rhythm. His arm slides underneath and holds my hips in place as he hammers against me. He's usually so gentle but this fierce, untamed version of Luke is turning me on in a whole new way. It's all I can do to hang on for the ride, as he takes me hard, pounding me to a fast, sweaty orgasm.

It doesn't roll through me like a wave, rather it slams into me and leaves me panting after it's over. He cries out and by the quick jerk of his hips and how his shoulders bunch and flex beneath my fingers, I know he's come, too. I hold him against me, not ready to let him go just yet. But when I try to pull back, he tightens his arms around me. He shudders again and turns his head away and my heart breaks all over again.

All I can do is hold the man I love close and pretend not to feel the moisture leaking onto my shoulder.

———

Over the next few weeks, things seem better. I send my landlord two months' rent in exchange for breaking my lease and arrange for movers to pack up my apartment. It's odd to be making these sorts of changes but I'm determined to go forward with purpose. No more sticking my head in the sand or avoiding hard decisions.

Luke wants me to stay and there's nowhere I want to be more than here. He needs me. And I need him, too.

He's been spending a lot of time on his coding initiative. I think it's just an excuse to take his mind off things but I wholeheartedly approve of anything that focuses his mind on something productive.

We spend hours each day debating ideas and brainstorming. At times he seems almost like the old Luke. Brilliant and creative and driven.

At other times he seems like a mere shadow.

He's gone to help Tank set up his new stereo system, something I suspect is just his brother's way of checking up on him. If I didn't already like his brothers, I would absolutely adore them by now. Every day someone has found a reason to stop by and see him.

Luke doesn't know how to ask for what he needs, so the fact that they're coming to him shows how well they know him. And how much they care for him. Even though Luke often feels like the odd one out since he didn't grow up with any of them, it's equally as obvious that they're determined to include him in their lives going forward.

Something I'm grateful for.

Things have been so hectic around here that I've missed my last two calls with Grace. I've been emailing her to let her know what's going on but it's not the same as hearing her voice. I settle on the couch and call her. As usual she answers right away. When she hears my voice, the music in the background immediately lowers.

"Hey. How are things going? Is Luke doing any better?"

I didn't tell Grace the whole story but she's aware that Luke's been having a hard time dealing with his father's death. She still doesn't know about my role in things.

"Better. Much better. I'm so sorry I couldn't call before."

"It's fine. I totally understand."

"I just didn't want you to think I forgot about you. Things have just been so messed up here."

"Whoa, Sev. What's going on? I've never heard you so upset before."

I sniffle, trying to rein in my emotions. It's been an emotional few weeks. And now I have to admit to her that after all the promises I've made, I'm probably not going to get custody of her after all. Agent Walker hasn't contacted me again but since the raid went so wrong, I seriously doubt if he's going to be anxious to help me. Truthfully, I'm just trying to stay off his radar completely.

"I did something. Something I'm not proud of."

Grace doesn't interrupt for once but I can hear her breathing on the other end so I know she's listening.

"At the time I told myself I had a good reason. It was so I could push my petition for custody through. I was worried that I wouldn't be approved otherwise. Now it's all ruined anyway so you'll have to stay with the Barnetts a little longer until I can figure something else out. I'm so sorry, Grace."

I take a deep breath. It was hard to admit my mistakes but I feel better now that she knows. It's disappointing but I just want her to know that I haven't given up on her. That I'll never leave her to fend for herself, the way I had to.

She sighs.

"Seven ... I've been trying to figure out how to tell you this for months now. The Barnetts have actually said that they ... they want to adopt me."

"They do?"

Even though it's a great thing and I should be happy for her I can't deny that I feel a little lost hearing this. Through everything I've always thought of Grace and I being together again one day. A real family. Now she's going to be family with someone else.

"I was afraid to tell you."

Now I'm ashamed. She's had the opportunity to have some stability in her life and she's been holding off out of fear of hurting me. Again, somehow I've managed to make it all about me when it's supposed to be the other way around.

"Oh Grace. You shouldn't have to be afraid of anything. All I've ever wanted is for you to be happy."

"It's just that you've always worked so hard trying to figure out a way for us to be together. And I'm just here living a normal teenage life. Without you. When they told me they wanted to adopt me, I felt so guilty for being happy when you're still alone."

Her voice is so small that she sounds like a little girl again. Maybe that's my problem. In my head she's forever that abandoned baby and I haven't been ready to see that she's growing up. It's time for both of us to move on.

"We've both been feeling guilty for wanting to live our lives. But maybe this is how things are meant to be. You'll always be my sister, Grace. No matter what."

"Promise?"

"I promise. Go tell the Barnetts that you're ready to get adopted."

She sniffles a little on the other end of the line. "Okay. But wait, what about you? Does this mean that you're going to stay with the hottie hacker now?"

"Yes. He asked me to stay. He really loves me Grace. And I love him, too. I just hate that I'll be so far away from you."

"I'll miss you, too but don't worry about me. Luke is the one who needs you right now."

"I'm not sure what he needs."

"Seven, he's never lost a parent before. *You have.* You'd know better than anyone what he needs right now."

After we hang up, I think about what she said. When I lost my mom, for years all I could think about was why. That's how I know Luke is torturing himself with guilt over what happened. I pick up my cell phone again and start dialing.

My sister is right. I know *exactly* what he needs.

———

I open the door and allow Tank to come in. A few minutes later Gabe and Zack arrive together. They all take seats on the couch. I glance behind me to make sure that Luke isn't out of the shower yet.

"We're just waiting on—"

Finn pokes his head through the door. "Am I late?"

I usher him inside and to the chair I pulled from the kitchen. "Right on time. He'll be out in a second."

Sure enough, a few minutes later Luke emerges wearing a pair of jeans unsnapped at the waist. His hair is still wet, the thick curls gleaming in the light.

"When did you guys get here?" He manages an appropriate amount of interest when he asks the question. Someone who didn't know him well might not be able to tell that anything is wrong but I can hear the trepidation in his voice.

He glances over at me warily.

"I asked them to come. So I can tell them the truth."

"Seven—"

"It's my fault. And you've been self-destructing this past month with guilt." He closes his eyes. "You've been trying to hide it but it's so obvious. I know you blame me."

"I don't blame you. I blame myself. Never you."

Tank turns to me. "You mentioned over the phone that Luke gave information to the authorities about Max?"

"Yeah, but he only did it to save me. They were threatening to arrest me if I didn't help them get information from Luke. So he gave them some information he thought wouldn't implicate Max directly but I guess it did somehow. We never thought this would happen."

"Of course you didn't. Why would you?" Tank replies. His eyes shift over to Luke. "Do you know what my most vivid memory is of Max? It's watching the lights on his car as he drove away when he left us. I can still hear my mom crying."

Luke sits on the edge of the couch but doesn't say anything.

Tank looks over at Finn. "Do you even remember that?"

Finn shakes his head. "I have no conscious memories from that age. And when we met again, I didn't care about getting to know him at all. I just figured if some old guy wanted to give out money, why not let him?"

Luke looks up in shock.

"What? You thought you were the only one with a fucked up relationship with our mafia pops?" Gabe chuckles. "I stole his assistant's security card so I could snoop around his hotel suite."

"Yeah, you showed me the pictures you took." Luke smiles. "I had forgotten that."

Gabe holds his ribs. "I haven't forgotten any of that. I still can't twist my torso without feeling it where that crazy bastard knifed me."

"Your father stabbed you?" I blurt, forgetting that I'm supposed to be an impartial observer.

Zack chuckles at my outburst. "No, that would be our mafia hitman cousin, Blade. Apparently Max helped raise him though, so I'm not sure that's much better."

Luke crosses his arm. "So the point is that we've all had some pretty insane interactions with Max."

Zack pats him on the shoulder. "I told him everything he did wrong. I accused him of being selfish, irresponsible and fucking up all our lives. He let me, too. Our relationship wasn't puppies and rainbows. It was ninety-nine percent me yelling at him for being a shitty father."

They fall quiet. Finally Luke sighs. "You guys didn't have to come over here just to make me feel better."

Tank stands. "We didn't come over here to make you feel better. We're here to tell you that we feel responsible, too. But it's something we've had to come to terms with. Did you ever get a chance to talk to him, one on one?"

Luke nods thoughtfully. "The day I warned him about what was coming, we had lunch together. He was so different from what I was expecting. In my head I'd built him up to be this monster but in the end, he was just a man."

"Max would have been the first to admit that he wasn't a great person for most of his life. He wasn't arrested unjustly. It's probably a miracle he evaded authorities as long as he did. It wasn't your fault, Luke. You just accelerated the inevitable."

Tank pulls him into a hug and I hang back watching them. Soon conversation turns to other things and slowly, Luke starts to sound more like himself.

After an hour, Tank looks at his watch and then stands. "I'd better go. If I don't come home with the right flavor of ice cream, Em is going to kill me. Oh by the way, you're all going to be uncles soon."

There's a chorus of cheers and what looks like a lot of pushing and shoving but at the end they're all grinning so I assume this is part of how they bond. They all file out and I wave to them one by one. Finally only Tank is left.

"We were getting worried about you, kid."

Luke crosses his arms. "I know. Thank you for this. Seriously, I needed to hear some of that. I'll probably always feel guilty for how things went down but it helps to put things in perspective. He was a terrible father in so many ways but at the end he was making an effort to redeem himself. I'll have to come to terms with that in my own time so I can move on and forgive him."

Tank claps him on the shoulder. "Maybe then you can finally forgive yourself."

Chapter Nineteen

Luke

*V*oices and music carry over the warm afternoon air from the backyard of my mom's house. It's the end of the summer and this will probably be the last cookout of the season.

I sit on the front steps and sigh as I'm finally alone. My family has been worried about me and I know I've given them reason but it's almost as exhausting to have them all hovering. Thank God for Seven.

Just the thought of my girl brings a smile to my face.

Her love and patience have been a balm to my ragged soul. As the days pass and I love her deeper still, I can feel the wounds in my heart starting to heal.

She has moved in completely and my living room has become her office. My apartment never seemed small before but now that we're both living and working from the same space, it suddenly feels microscopic. My brothers know more about real estate than I do so they've been keeping an eye out for property we might want to buy. Just a few months ago the idea of buying land and living with someone would have freaked me out but now I wouldn't have it any other way.

Seven's laughter carries over the sound of the music. I was worried that after years alone that she'd think it was weird to spend so much time with my mom or resent having to entertain my grandpop and my overly friendly uncles. But she fit right in from the very first time she met everyone. I think they get along better with her sometimes than with me!

A delivery truck pulls up to the curb and the driver jumps out. Whistling, he makes his way up the driveway, a parcel in his hand.

"Luke Marshall?" he asks.

I stand. "That's me."

He holds out his clipboard for me to sign and then once I'm done, hands me the large padded envelope. "Have a great day!"

I don't respond, my mind already on the contents of the envelope. Not just on the contents but on the fact that it was delivered here. I haven't gotten mail at my mom's place in ages. I don't recognize the sender but when I rip it open, I immediately recognize the distinctive blue paper inside. With trembling hands, I unfold the letter. It's dated over a month ago.

Dear Luke,

Writing this letter is one of the hardest things I've ever done. But I feel that in death a man should be able to set things right. Though nothing can ever atone for the things I've done, I want to try. I'll start with an apology.

I am truly sorry for all the pain I've caused.

Your mother is a beautiful, strong, spirited woman and I loved her even though I had no right to. She has raised you to be a man of integrity and honor. Because of this I know that you will be looking back on our last interaction with sadness or even guilt. But any guilt you have, I ask now that you let it go.

My son, things happen the way they are meant to. I could never be angry with you for anything. I've watched you grow from afar these many years and I hope one day, perhaps when you have children of your own, that you can understand a fraction of how much I've loved you. Or that you'll at least be able to look back and remember me without anger.

So many emotions bounce around inside of me as I read my father's final words. Guilt, sadness, shame, weakness. I've been eaten up by guilt and self-recrimination but I see now that Max wouldn't have wanted that. He had his faults but he wanted me to be happy. My heart lighter, I pick up reading where I left off.

What I wish most is for you to go forward with the knowledge that I am at peace. That's all a man can ask for in this life though I do have one final request.

Live. Live well. For life only happens once.

And now I leave you my son with a bit of Irish wisdom.

Go bhfana í ngrá linn,
Iad siúd atá í ngrá linn.
Iad siúd nach bhfuil,
Go gcasa Dia a gcroíthe.
Agus muna gcasann Sé a gcroíthe
Go gcasa Sé caol na coise acu
Go n-aithneoimid iad as a mbacadaíl.

May those who love us,
Love us.
And those who do not love us,
May God turn their hearts.

And if He doesn't turn their hearts,
May He turn their ankles,
So we'll know them by their limping.

With love,

Maxwell Marshall

While I was on the verge of embarrassing myself by crying right here in the open when I read the last stanza, I burst into laughter. The sound rolls through me, erasing weeks of guilt and doubt.

"You always have to get the last word, don't you?" I look up to the sky as I ask the question. Who knows, maybe he can hear me.

It's too late for us to have a relationship but it's not too late for me to heed his advice. That's the ultimate way to honor my father's legacy. Despite his faults, he sacrificed quite a bit so that we could live free from the burdens of his past. To give us a life that was our own.

The least I can do is live that life to the fullest.

"What are you doing sitting out here, sweetie? You'd better get back in there before your Uncle Eddie eats all of that apple pie."

My mom comes out of the front door and then lowers herself to the step beside me.

Without a word, I hand her the letter. She reads it silently, stopping halfway through to wipe away tears. She folds it carefully and hands it back.

"He was always a good man underneath. Troubled but a good man. I'm glad I wasn't wrong about that."

I turn to look at her. When I was too young to know better, I used to ask about my father all the time. But once I was old enough to understand I avoided any mention of him, wanting to spare her embarrassment or pain. But now with a little distance, I wonder if that was a mistake. Maybe I would have understood him better, and her better, too if I'd asked a few more questions. Or at least tried to understand what drew them together in the first place instead of just casting Max as a villain without a care.

"How did you do it, Mom? Over the years, you never made me feel like I was a burden even though I know it had to have been hard. I was a constant reminder of him."

She puts her arm around my shoulders. "It was hard but it was never a burden. You're the best thing that ever happened to me. You're not a reminder of your father. You're a gift."

"I can only hope to be half the parent you were one day. But you set the bar awfully high."

She smiles, delighted. "Oh sweetheart. I can't wait for that day either. Speaking of babies ..."

"Here we go." I chuckle at my own stupidity for even giving her the opening. She's been hinting rather heavily lately that I should make sure Seven knows how much I respect her and that I don't just want to *live in sin* as she calls it. I didn't want to tell her that Sev and I are both quite enjoying living in sin. And sinning as often as we can.

"That sweet girl is mighty worried about you. I am, too."

I hold up the letter. "I'm going to be fine now but I guess I should get back inside so she can see that. She's been amazing through all of this."

"She loves you."

"I love her, too. I just wish I could do something for her. To show her how I feel."

Mom pats my shoulder as she stands up. "You'll think of something. Now come on because I'm not making another one of those pies!"

Before I go back in the house, I stash my father's letter in my back pocket. My uncles and cousins tend to be pretty nosy and I'm not ready for anyone else to read those words yet. Except for my girl, that is.

I find Seven in the kitchen standing guard over the last slice of pie. She's holding a fork out like a weapon. My uncle Eddie stands on the other side of the counter eyeing it like he's looking for a weak spot in her defense.

"Stand back. I have no problem fighting an old man," she threatens.

He laughs. "Come on. If he hasn't come back by now, he isn't coming. I won't tell him."

"Uncle Eddie, are you trying to steal my girl?"

He makes a disgruntled face when I reach over and grab the plate. He winks at Seven. "I was trying to steal the pie but the girl is a close second. You're lucky she saved it for you. You've got a good one here, Luke."

My eyes meet hers. "Yeah, I know."

Uncle Eddie satisfies himself with several chocolate chip cookies and then shuffles out. Finally we're alone.

"Do you feel better? It was kind of loud earlier, huh?"

I swallow a forkful of pie. She really is a good one. Plenty of girls would be pissed if their boyfriend left them to fend for themselves at a family event but Sev gets it when I need a moment of solitude. There are no questions or accusations. Just understanding.

I pull my father's letter from my back pocket. "While I was out there, this arrived."

Her mouth falls open slightly as she reads. When she's done, she folds it carefully and hands it back. "Wow. Are you okay after reading that?"

"Actually ... yeah. Max was at peace and that's all I can ask for. I'll always wish that I could have spent a little more time with him though."

The thought brings to mind the perfect gift for Seven. The one thing she's always wanted. Her sister.

I walk around the counter and hug her from behind.

"You know, I didn't give the FBI everything."

She tenses against me. "Luke—"

"No, just hear me out. Now that Max is gone, I'm not worried about holding anything back. If we bargain right, we could probably get custody of your sister. Dealing with Agent Walker will be a pain but we can do it. I know how much that means to you. I want you to have everything you need to be happy."

She turns in my arms and kisses me gently. "I do have every-thing I need. Right here."

"But what about Grace?"

"She told me she's happy where she is. And I'm finally happy, too."

Even though she seems sincere, I worry that she's brushing aside things that matter to her to be with me.

"You don't have to pretend that you're not disappointed. I know how much the custody petition meant to you. Maybe if we get married it'll give your petition more weight. I'm a billionaire and money speaks. We don't have to just let this go."

She covers my mouth with her hand. "Don't call the cavalry yet. Grace is fine. She told me she's happy where she is. The family she's fostering with wants to adopt her and I think it's for the best."

Slightly mollified, I nip at the back of her hand. "If you're sure. Well, maybe I'll buy a helicopter so you can visit her whenever you want. I'm a billionaire after all."

She laughs. "You're a billionaire, huh? I didn't catch that."

We laugh together, mocking the media firestorm that has turned our lives upside down. My father's dramatic death in police custody brought an insane amount of attention to our family. Social media in particular went crazy with the discovery of five young billionaires. Gabe has become especially popular. There's a Twitter account devoted just to his *hair*.

I've started texting the memes to him every day just because it annoys him so much.

"Sev?"

"Hmm?"

"I wanted to say thank you. For loving me. Sticking with me this past month and giving me the space I needed to work things out in my own head. I know that couldn't have been easy but you were always there when I needed you."

"And I always will be."

"I'm so glad I didn't listen to my mom when I was a kid."

"What do you mean?" She crinkles her nose at the seemingly sudden change of topic.

"She always told me not to talk to strangers online."

I kiss her until she throws her arms around my neck and we're both gasping for breath. When she finally opens her eyes, her expression is dreamy. I hope to keep that look on her face for the rest of her life.

Chapter Twenty

Seven

One year later ...

I pick up a piece of bubble wrap and carefully pack it around a coffee mug. We're going to be moving into our new house this weekend.

I look around the apartment which is in varying stages of being dismantled. There are white squares on the wall where Luke took down pictures and the living room floor is covered in boxes and that fluffy white packing material that looks like popcorn.

It's going to be so weird not to wake up here anymore. This apartment has been the place our love has grown. Where I finally stopped worrying this won't work out or that Luke will get bored and find someone better.

It's home in a way nowhere else has ever been.

Even though there are packing materials all over the place, we've both been so busy that we haven't put much *inside* the boxes yet. Luke wanted to hire movers to handle it all but I told him it wasn't necessary. Now that I'm with one of the country's most eligible young bachelors, I'm more aware of the difference in our financial status than ever. Luke knows I don't care about the size of his bank account but I don't want to be seen as *that girl*.

Luckily I have a whole new group of "sisters" to help me navigate this strange new world. Emma warned me that dealing with the other side of wealth is an inevitability so at least I was prepared before the first unflattering tabloid article came out.

I spent an evening sloppy drunk on Emma's couch while Sasha spoon-fed us both ice cream after I saw it but now all that crap rolls right off my back. There will always be people making assumptions about our relationship or musing about why he's with a skinny, scarred girl but I refuse to let that stuff bother me. Luke loves me and thinks I'm perfect exactly as I am. His opinion is the only one I care to listen to anyway.

Luke emerges from the bedroom and stops when he sees me packing. "Baby, why didn't you call me to help? I don't want you doing all this alone."

He kneels next to me and grabs the duct tape. I hold the sides of the box together while he seals it.

"Did I tell you that another school signed up for the program?" He does a little victory dance. He's so goofy sometimes and I love it. After seeing him so despondent, it's been a joy to watch him return to his usual playful, happy disposition. My Luke is back.

"That's awesome. You've got almost the entire state covered."

"Yeah. Your plan to use existing schools was brilliant."

For months, we were spinning our wheels about how to get things off the ground. Luke's original proposal called for funding the construction of our own buildings. Then I got the idea to approach school systems about either integrating our classes into their existing curriculum or offering them as an extracurricular activity. I figured a few would go for the idea but the response was overwhelming. So many schools signed up that Luke had to hire a program director just to handle all the paperwork.

Using existing infrastructure has not only saved money but solved the transportation issue. Most of the school systems already have busing in place for kids involved in after-school activities. And holding the coding classes on school grounds has ensured that they remain a safe space for children to learn.

That's going down as one of my best ideas yet.

"I am pretty brilliant, aren't I?" Brushing dust off my jeans, I sit on the couch and rest my head against the cushions.

"I'm smart enough to know a trick question when I hear one," he responds absently, absorbed by whatever he's looking at on his phone.

Suddenly, he breaks out into a huge grin and then vaults over the arm of the couch onto the cushion next to me. "Hey, why didn't you tell me?"

"Tell you what?"

He holds out his phone. "That your newest game is doing so well."

"What? Let me see." I grab the phone from his hand and then squeal at the top of my lungs. "My game is number one. I'm number one!"

He laughs and pulls me into a kiss. "*Pig Punt in Paradise* is number one. That's something to tell our kids someday."

Even in the middle of my excitement, his words give me pause. He's been doing that more and more lately. Making references to the future that include things we haven't really talked about yet like kids and mortgages and family vacations. I figure he's just trying the ideas on for size, seeing how they fit. But every time he mentions something like that a warm feeling of contentment settles around me.

"Are you going to call your sister? Or do you want to wait and tell her in person?"

"I think I'll tell her next time we visit. She's always good for a dramatic reaction."

Once Grace wasn't worried about me feeling left out, she stopped acting out and has gotten involved in several clubs at school. Her adoption went through a few months ago and we've gone to visit her in New Jersey a few times. Unlike what I was expecting, Jim and Enid Barnett weren't just fostering Grace for money. They really love her.

It was bittersweet to watch her with her new parents. Once they knew I wasn't a threat to their adoption of Grace, they were extremely open to more frequent visitation. I'm starting to think of them as extended family.

"Thanks for going with me to visit Grace, by the way. She really likes it when you come with me."

He gives me a wry look. "I can tell. She pinched my ass when she hugged me goodbye last time."

I stifle a smile. "Aw, poor baby. I'll make it up to you tonight."

His head dips and I shiver when his nose brushes against my neck. "I'm going to hold you to that."

After a loud, smacking kiss against my neck, he gets up and walks into the kitchen. "You didn't pack the coffee maker?"

I shake my head. "No, I figured that would be dangerous. I know how you get without caffeine. I'll unplug it and drive it over this weekend."

He stares at me for a long time. Then his expression softens in a way I've never seen. One side of his mouth lifts slightly. "Want some coffee, baby?"

"Yes. Please," I manage to get out.

What was that about? My cheeks flush as he finally turns away. He's *never* looked at me quite that way before. He disappears into our bedroom and then comes out a few minutes later. I watch as he pulls out a filter and measures the coffee. Then he retrieves his favorite *Star Wars* mug from the shelf. It's the only one I didn't pack yet since he uses it every day.

We don't speak as the coffee percolates and once it's finished, he prepares a single cup. One cream. Two sugars. Exactly the way I like it. He carries it to me and then kneels next to where I sit on the couch.

My heart is suddenly beating so fast, like it knows there's something special about this moment.

"Thank you." I accept the hot mug, smiling at him through the steam that curls above the rim.

Then he puts out his other hand. On his palm is a diamond ring. A simple solitaire on a gold band. Exactly what I would have chosen for myself.

He smiles sheepishly. "I always said if I did this, it would be over coffee."

My breath whooshes out and I take the ring from his hand with shaking fingers. "This? What is *this* exactly?"

"A promise." He kisses me, the steam from the coffee warming our lips. "That I'll love you forever. Marry me, Seven?"

I place the mug down on the table and then pull him closer. My throat is suddenly very tight. "Yes. *Yes!* There's nothing I want more than to be with you."

"That's what I want, too." His finger brushes back and forth over my cheek. "To be your one person to call. Your one person to love. Forever."

Now I understand what it means when people say they're brimming with emotion. I feel like a coffee cup that's running over, my love for him spilling all over us both.

"All those years ago when you said you'd be my one person to call, did you ever think we'd end up here?"

He shakes his head. "Honestly, I figured we'd both end up in jail. But this is a different kind of life sentence."

Our laughter fills the apartment, the joyous sound echoing everything I'm feeling inside. I've found my person.

Forever.

Chapter Twenty-One

Luke

My eyes follow the curve of Seven's ass as she moves around our new kitchen. It's amazing that she only gets more beautiful as time passes. When she stretches up to reach for something in one of the cabinets, I curl a hand around her hip. When she sees the look in my eyes, she gasps.

"Luke! Your whole family is here." She dissolves into giggles when I corner her, bracketing her against the counter with my hips.

"You're my wife now. They expect me to feel you up."

It still feels surreal to call her my wife. We got married in a private ceremony with just our close family and friends a month after I proposed. That might seem fast to some people but Sev has spent her entire life feeling unwanted. And I plan to make sure she never feels that way again.

"I'm sure your brothers don't want to see that," she responds patiently.

"Why are they here again? Can we get rid of them?" I whisper, kissing her behind the ear.

She's been baking all morning, with my mom's help, and she smells warm like sugar. I lick delicately at her neck and she shivers.

"They're here to help us celebrate our new house. We can't kick them out when we're the ones who invited them." Her hands slide up my chest and pull me closer. "Maybe we can sneak away later?"

"Hey guys! Oops—" Sasha spins in mid-step and walks back out of the kitchen.

Seven muffles her laughter against my shoulder. "We can't hide in the kitchen the whole time. It's a party."

"*This* is a party." I pop her on the bottom. She rubs up against me, one hand sliding into my hair.

"Is it safe to come in?" Tank sticks his head in the kitchen, the smug grin on his face telling me he knows exactly what we were just up to.

"No, it's not."

But Seven ducks under my arm and rushes toward Tank. Well, toward the gorgeous baby he's holding.

"Max! Oh my god, she's gotten so big."

Tank allows her to take the baby without complaint. His daughter, Maxine, is frequently the main attraction at family events and he's used to being forced to give her up as soon as he walks in.

"How old is she now?" I ask, laughing when Seven takes the baby's socks off. She's recently developed an obsession with baby feet.

Even I have to admit it's pretty hard to resist squeezing those chubby little toes.

"Ten months. Emma's getting the rest of her stuff from the car. Now that she's walking we have to travel with a truck-load of safety crap to keep her from falling down stairs or sticking forks in the electric sockets."

"Tank! What did you just say?"

Emma appears carrying a baby gate. I take it from her and place it between the kitchen and the living room. I know the drill. We'll move it around from room to room to keep the baby contained.

"Nothing, baby. Do you need any help setting anything up?"

Emma shakes her head. "I've got it. Sasha got here early to set up so I wouldn't have to."

Seven glances over. "Thank you again for planning this party for us, Em. If it was up to Luke and me, we'd probably be eating hot dogs."

Emma sits next to Tank at our long breakfast banquette table. "Anything for you, sis. I'm just going to sit for a minute."

I stroke a gentle finger over baby Max's cheek as she gnaws on Seven's shoulder. "She's so cute."

"Cute and obviously keeping her parents up all night. I think we should offer to babysit again," Sev whispers and nods her head toward the table.

Emma is fast asleep with her head cradled on her arms. Next to her, Tank is slumped in the corner, his head resting on the wall behind him as he snores softly.

"Wow. I think that's a new record."

"I know. Poor things. Oh, can you get the mail? I'm so used to living in apartments and just grabbing the mail on the way into the building. I haven't checked the mail in three days!"

I can't even tease her since I'm guilty of the same thing. Living in a house has been quite an adjustment, especially one that's this big. Originally, we wanted to just buy something already constructed but due to our new security requirements, we ended up building something new.

It's so big I feel like an idiot getting lost in my own house sometimes but it has tons of land for the two labrador retriever pups Emma convinced us to adopt and a crazy high security fence. The mailbox is all the way at the end of our long driveway.

"Sure thing. I'll be back."

Mounds of presents explode off the table in the hallway and just in case anyone missed it, there's a massive *House-warming Party* banner hanging over it. I shake my head. It's easy to see my sister-in-law's influence. Emma loves a grand statement.

I pass the living room and raise my hand in greeting when Gabe and Zack look up. They're helping one of my young cousins put together a model car. Through the back window I can see Finn and Rissa relaxing on our wraparound porch. My mom sits on the couch looking out the window, the widower she's been dating recently sitting next to her looking uncomfortable.

I grin. He's probably uncomfortable because he was greeted by my security team when he arrived. My very big and scary security team. Tank recommended his old employer, Alexander Security, and they've been great. Professional but completely unobtrusive. I only notice them when I need them which luckily isn't often.

Our circular drive is filled with cars so I walk directly across the grass to the end of the lawn. Our mailbox is double-sided and mounted into the security gate. I pull it open and then pick up the stack of letters inside. Something flutters out and lands at my feet.

It's a feather.

I stoop and pick it up. It's a deep red color and large in size. It looks much too large to belong to any of the birds I've seen in the area.

A chill runs up my spine.

"You're a crazy old bird, you know that?"

"I'll take that as a compliment. I always thought of myself as a phoenix. A fighter that rises from the ashes of its own demise."

I glance behind me at the mailbox and then around the expansive yard. Our drive is bordered by trees and the summer sun overhead beats down mercilessly, making me grateful for the shade. Maybe I should feel worried being out in the open but I'm not. Instead I'm comforted. I rub the feather between my fingers.

"Rise, Max. Rise. And be at peace."

I must have been standing here longer than I thought because when I look up next I see Seven walking down the drive toward me, her long black hair whipping behind her in the breeze. She waves her hand at me.

"Babe, I thought you got kidnapped out here. I was about to send out the hounds to protect you."

She looks down affectionately at the two puppies gamboling around her feet. Loki falls over a stick and then whips around to attack it. Uninterested in his brother's drama, Anakin races over to me and then flops his bottom directly on top of my shoe. His large tongue lolls out of the side of his mouth, a look of complete doggy happiness on his face.

"Yeah, they're really scary."

She bends down and scratches Loki under his chin. "Don't listen to Daddy. You're a big, scary hound."

I pick up Anakin and we walk back up the driveway, my mind still reeling from my discovery.

"You're so quiet. Everything okay?" She looks over at me and she's so damn beautiful it almost breaks my heart.

Beautiful and all mine.

"Yeah. Everything is perfect now."

That's when she spies the red feather in my hand. She stretches out her hand to touch it, trailing a finger over the length. "Pretty. Where'd you find that?"

I gesture over my shoulder.

"In the mailbox?" she asks in disbelief. "Like a bird crawled in there just to leave this for us? That's so strange."

I tuck the feather into my back pocket for safekeeping. "Crazy old birds do strange things sometimes."

Then I follow the love of my life back inside the home we've made together and toward a future that suddenly seems brighter than ever.

The End

... at last

Thank you so much for reading *Luke*.

Bonus Material: Want to read about Tank's bachelor

party? It's available as a bonus story for my VIP list members. Sign up HERE.

Ready for more billionaire romance?

My parents just put a gold diggers target on my back. But if all they want is a wedding, I can do that. I'll find the fiancee of their nightmares. *Who Wants to Marry a Billionaire? Must be completely inappropriate.* **Download Bad King now!**

If you're in the mood for a really inappropriate romantic comedy, then **One-click BEG ME now!** Find out what happens when a hotshot ad executive discovers his rooster will only crow for one woman. His competition.

Keep reading for an excerpt of BEG ME!

The universe clearly hates me.

I work hard and I like to win. So of course, the only woman that gets me going these days is the one woman I need to avoid like the plague. My co-worker. Rival, she-devil and my competition for the biggest ad account this side of the Atlantic.

When I find out she's never taken a trip to O-town, we make a little wager. Not only will I win the client, but I'll prove to her that multiple O's are not a myth.

We work together all day and fight between the sheets all night. But somewhere along the way, I discover that winning isn't enough.

Excerpt of *Beg Me* © 2018 M. Malone

MILO

Time to get our game faces on.

As we approach the table, everyone stands, and the introductions are made all around. Maybe it's because I'm watching Mr. Lavin so closely that I see how his eyes follow Mya after she shakes his hand and then walks around the table to greet the other members of his team. She knows all of their names, as do I. Then she takes a seat right next to me.

Before I can even sit down, James is already ordering a scotch from the waitress. Then I see why.

Elizabeth is sitting two tables away.

She raises her glass of wine in our direction. I turn to see James give a begrudging wave. I'm not sure if anyone else has noticed her yet, but she's already accomplished her goal. There's no way James can focus completely on the client tonight with his ex-wife sitting right in his line of vision.

Christ.

"Thank you all for traveling to meet with me. I've had this week scheduled with potential investors for months, so it's been helpful that you could come to me while I'm already in the States."

"When do you go back to Italy?" Wallace asks. "I follow you on Instagram. You guys, his page is *lit*. Fast cars, beautiful clothes. You're living the dream, man." He sighs before digging into his salad course enthusiastically.

Andre just laughs. "Thank you. This is our goal, to be as the kids say, *fire*. Why is all of the American slang centered around temperature, I wonder? It used to be that things were *cool*, now they're *hot, fire, bomb* or *lit*. Fascinating. I have an entire team of people who study the social media trends."

James looks like he has no idea what is happening. But I strongly suspect that Wallace in his own unique, bumbling way has just broken the ice for us.

Well, if he's broken the ice, I might as well jump in first. "Mirage employs a lot of talented young designers. It's why our ad campaigns are so on trend. We combine years of experience in understanding what makes people buy with the fresh perspective of different generations."

Mya grins over at me. "Wallace is on Milo's team. He's been with us for almost a year now and graduated from Columbia with honors. He's also an amateur photographer and is pretty popular on Instagram, too."

I glance over at her. *He is?* How does she know all that? Maybe there is something to paying attention in those bullshit icebreaker sessions at work after all.

Wallace looks shocked, too. "My account has nowhere near the numbers some of my friends have, but I just passed ten thousand."

Mr. Lavin actually looks impressed. "That's quite an accomplishment, especially for a hobbyist." He clears his throat. "I'm happy to meet with you all in person after hearing about you from Mr. Lawson."

James gives him a tight smile. "I'm extremely proud of my team."

"It shows," Andre replies.

Dinner proceeds with the typical pleasantries. Wallace looks a little confused, but I can only pray the kid can hold his tongue. With these types of clients, you never rush right into business. You need to woo them, almost like a woman you're trying to convince to come back to your place after dinner. She's not just going to come with you if you ask within the first ten minutes. She needs you to show her that you're worth her time. Are you going to savor her the same way you do the ten-inch porterhouse on your plate? Or will you rush through the act like a kid scarfing down an ice cream cone?

I can't imagine a man like Andre Lavin scarfing anything. He needs to see that we're not only the best team to take over his marketing but also that we're people he can work with.

We need him to *like* us.

As the waitress is clearing the entrees, Andre looks around the table with satisfaction. "Perhaps it is old-fashioned, but I care to meet with any agencies that work on our marketing directly. It's important that the people crafting our image understand what we're about here at Lavin Fashions."

Everyone instantly ceases their side conversations and pays attention. Now we're getting to the good stuff. The reason we're all here.

"What is your vision of Lavin Fashions, Mr. Lavin?" Mya asks. "I've read the official company mission statement, but I would love to hear it from you."

"Please, call me Andre."

The way he's looking at her makes it seem like he just wants to hear her say his name. My hand sitting on top of the table curls into a fist. It's unsettling that this bothers me. He's just a client, throwing a little charm at the pretty ad executive.

I've seen it plenty of times, and I've had my fair share of clients, male and female, attempt to flirt with me.

None of those made me want to growl in frustration. Or made me worry that Mya might actually want to flirt back.

"It's much more than just the clothes," Andre begins after a brief pause. "Our brand creates the garments that become part of people's memories. And for our newest venture, we're looking for a partner that understands the importance of family, friendship, love."

The woman sitting next to him sniffs. *Cristiane Laveque.* From my research on the Lavin team, I know that she's a top designer for Lavin Fashions.

"Apologies, but this is not a strength of American companies, we have found. So few understand *l'amore.*" She shakes her head ruefully as if the vulgar ways of the American market are just too much.

Mentally, I'm rolling my eyes, but this could be a real obstacle to winning their business. If they think that we're not cultured enough, it will be difficult to change that opinion. Granted, Mirage does plenty of "American" commercials and brands, but it's not like we're all racecars and beer. We have plenty of upper-echelon brands in the jewelry, hotel and entertainment industries.

"I believe Mirage can handle anything. We have such a diverse workforce that all of our clients find someone they can relate to. We also have more women in leadership roles than many of our competitors."

Maybe that'll calm her fears that we don't get *l'amore*. Mya in particular handles a lot of brands that cater to women, including a high-profile lingerie line.

Andre sits back in his chair and seems to be considering her words. "I must admit we've been approached by other firms that are run by people who are married. They understand what brides want."

James sits up straighter. "So, it is a bridal line?"

Andre laughs lightly. "Yes, the rumors are true. Lavin Fashions will introduce a new line called Lavin Bridal next year. It will be a separate division of the company which is why I'm meeting with investors. I didn't want word to get out until it was all finalized."

James looks like he's going to be sick. This is why Elizabeth has been so smug. She must have heard the Lavin group wanted someone who has been through the process of planning a wedding. Just another way for her to rub her recent marriage in James's face.

"I'm sure all the women on our team have mentally planned their dream wedding, even if they aren't married." I send a panicked glance at Mya.

This would be a really good fucking time for her to pipe in with some story of how she's been dreaming of her wedding dress since she was a little girl.

Unfortunately, Andre seems to be following my line of thought because he turns directly to Mya, too. "If you were planning a wedding, for example," he says, "wouldn't you want a wedding planner who was married?"

Mya pauses with her water glass halfway to her mouth. "Well, yes. I suppose I would."

James just blinks. Wallace pauses mid-chew with a piece of iceberg lettuce hanging from his lip. The whole table seems stunned into silence. She didn't mean to say that, and everyone can see it on her face. But in a rare, caught-off-guard moment, Mya has done the unforgivable.

She's been honest.

An awkward silence descends over the table. James takes another gulp from his scotch. Across from me, members of the Lavin team exchange significant glances before taking an interest in their plates. Worst of all, Andre Lavin just looks amused.

While Mya looks devastated.

You know how sometimes you can look back and identify the precise moment you fucked up? Well, later tonight I'm sure I'll be remembering the exact second I pushed us all off the cliff together.

"I agree," I state loudly.

James chokes slightly, and Wallace pounds him on the back. I ignore his panicked look and keep my eyes on Mr. Lavin.

"I agree with Mya," I repeat in case anyone at the table missed it the first time I pushed my career in front of a bus. "Having a married wedding planner would be great. Although I'd be more concerned about the people actually doing the work. That's really what sets Mirage apart."

By now, everyone is staring at me, especially James, probably wondering where the hell I'm going with this.

Mya, however, is watching me with a small, tremulous smile on her face. Like she can't believe that I'm backing her up right now. And damn if that smile isn't what does me in. Because I don't just bet on distracting Mr. Lavin; I double down and take it all the way to the bank.

"Mirage is really the best fit for anything to do with weddings. After all, it's the only agency I know with two team leads that are in love and engaged to be married." I turn to Mya and whisper, "Just go with it."

Then I tilt my head slightly and brush my lips over hers.

MYA

Everyone is staring. I can feel the heat of their eyes on the side of my face. But even that isn't enough to take me out of this moment. This sweet, thrilling moment. My eyes drift closed, and the world falls away.

Milo is kissing me.

If you'd asked me just an hour ago what kind of kisser I thought Milo would be, I'd have said aggressive. He's all about going all-in and getting to the finish line. I would have assumed that he wouldn't care much about the process but rather only about the end game.

I would have been completely and utterly wrong.

His lips are soft, and he feathers them over mine gently, barely touching me. The result is a whispery soft touch that sends chills up and down my spine. Then he lays his mouth over mine and kisses me properly, his tongue brushing softly against mine.

After what feels like several hours but is probably only several seconds, he pulls back. But he doesn't just stop. No, Milo can't do anything simply, not even shocking me to my core with a kiss. Because right after he pulls away, he does this soft little nuzzle, rubbing his nose back and forth against mine.

Why is that my kryptonite? That completely unnecessary little snuggle just takes all the indignation I was building up to and scatters it into the wind. Along with all rational thought.

A throat clears and it's like jumping into an ice bath. If we'd been standing, we'd have probably sprung apart, but instead I grope the table blindly until my hand connects with my water glass. The icy liquid cools my throat but not my lust.

What the hell was that?

Everyone at the table is still eating and talking softly amongst themselves, almost like the last thirty seconds didn't just change the rotational orbit of the planet. Isn't it funny how a certain event can knock you off your feet but seems to have no effect on anyone else? It's like experiencing an earthquake while everyone around you goes on with their lives unaware. Well, everyone isn't unaware. Andre Lavin is watching us carefully.

So is James.

Oh shit.

This is where I should speak up. Tell Mr. Lavin that I cannot wait to see his newest designs, that women everywhere are going to be clamoring for the chance to wear one of his dresses. But I can't because my mind is still muddled, and I can still feel the imprint of Milo's lips against mine.

"You make an interesting point, Mr. Hamilton. Being married is one thing, but to have a couple who are currently planning a wedding designing my campaign would be ideal." Mr. Lavin nods in satisfaction. "I had a good feeling about this firm, but I can see that your reputation is accurate. Professional, innovative and discreet. Exactly what I need."

James looks slightly dazed, the same expression you might wear after you narrowly miss being hit by a cab. He looks between me and Milo and then back to Mr. Lavin, but nothing comes out of his mouth.

Once again, Wallace comes to the rescue. "You can't go wrong with those two in charge, if you're looking for discretion. They've been dating in secret for ages and nobody knew except for me. I mean, I could tell. He stares at her ass whenever she walks away."

The water I just sipped comes back up my nose.

Milo hands me a napkin without missing a beat. "Thank you, Wallace. So, Mr. Lavin, tell us about your vision for Lavin

Bridal in particular."

And so it goes. Milo manages to carry the conversation all the way through the dessert course and then through coffee. Personally, I've never understood the practice of drinking coffee after dessert, but when the waitress comes around, I order some anyway. Maybe the extra caffeine will wake me the hell up.

But I still feel like I'm sleepwalking as James bids the members of the Lavin team goodnight and they promise to be in touch. Wallace is the first to scamper off, probably to go post the selfie he took with Mr. Lavin to Instagram. The thought makes me chuckle, but my throat instantly turns to sandpaper when James approaches.

This entire time, Milo and I have been sitting in silence. I couldn't take the chance of asking any questions where the Lavin team might overhear. But now I wish I'd thought to text him or something so I'd know how we're handling this.

But James doesn't look upset at all. He's practically glowing. It could be all the scotch, but either way, he looks thrilled.

"You two, ah, I should have known. You've done an amazing job keeping your relationship out of the office. Good work. Knew I could count on you." He claps Milo on the shoulder and gifts me with a wide, loopy grin.

Even if I knew what to say to him right now, I don't think I'd have the heart to wipe that smile off his face. Tomorrow is soon enough for him to realize that we've screwed up this deal. Maybe a good night's sleep will make him more lenient when he's deciding whether to fire us.

Milo pulls out my chair for me as I stand, and I follow wordlessly as we leave the restaurant. It's a Thursday night, but as we walk back through the casino to reach the elevators to the rooms, there are so many people out you'd never think it was a weekday. Time seems to move differently here. I notice an older lady with a purple fanny pack methodically feeding coins into a slot machine. She looks like she's been at it for a while. Maybe I should just stay down here, living off the free drinks and the adrenaline of gambling. It would probably be better than what's waiting for me when we get back to DC.

I'm so deep in my thoughts that I'm not paying attention when we get on the elevator. It's only when it stops that I realize we didn't push the button for my floor. But Milo loops his arm around my waist and guides me out of the elevator anyway.

"But my room–"

"Not here," he murmurs in my ear. The deep rumble of his voice so close sends a shiver down my spine. "Some of the Lavin team are on this floor. Wait until we get inside."

"Inside what?" Belatedly, I realize he means inside his room. He has his key card out and the door open before I can say, *No way in hell.*

The door slams shut behind us, and all the things I was getting ready to say get stuck in my throat.

Trying to gather my thoughts, I look around the room. The layout is the same as the one I was given, TV, big window directly across from the door, except he has a king-size bed instead of two doubles. Behind him, there are several dress shirts scattered on the bed, and the covers are all tangled, like he took a nap before coming down to dinner. Just like that I have a mental image of Milo naked in those sheets, and being alone with him in this room seems like a *very* bad idea.

Completely at ease with the idea of the two of us being alone, he shrugs out of his suit jacket and loosens his tie. I'm instantly distracted by the small patch of skin revealed at the top of his shirt where it's unbuttoned. "I know you must have a million questions," he says finally.

But I don't. Truthfully, I only have one.

"What the hell just happened?"

Download BEG ME now
at minxmalone.com/begme

gives him what he wants. *Her.*

All I Want: The only thing Kay wants is for Elliott Alexander to stop treating her like she's invisible. But a car accident forces her to reach out to the only man she trusts to save her.

All I Need is You : When the man she loves leaves town after their steamy kiss, Kaylee Wilhelm is done. But when she's targeted by a stalker, Eli is the only one who can protect her.

Just One Thing : Scientist Bennett Alexander is a bona fide genius but he still needs a dating tutor to "get the girl". What could go wrong? Other than falling for his teacher, of course!

The Simmons

Make Him Mine : Trent sees Mara Simmons as the little sister he never had. But she finally has a plan to get him exactly where he should be. *In her bed.*

Make Me Feel : Matt Simmons is over Army doctors until he sees his physical therapist is h-o-t. But Penny wants nothing to do with military men and Sgt. Sexy won't change her mind.

Make Her Stay : Mara has always known Trent is *The One.* But then she discovers the man she loves just might be a stranger.

Bad Business (The Kingsleys)

Bad King: My parents just put a gold diggers target on my back. But if all they want is a wedding, I can do that. I'll find the fiancee of their nightmares. *Who Wants to Marry a Billionaire? Must be completely inappropriate.*

Bad Blood : I'd do anything for my best friend's little sister. Until she asks for the one thing I can't give. One night. No rules. ***RITA® Award Winner!***

Blue-Collar Billionaires

Billions from the deadbeat dad they never knew sounds pretty sweet. Until they find out what he really wants.

Tank / Finn / Gabe / Zack / Luke

- Romantic Suspense -

Shameless / Force / Deep / Sin / Brazen

- Paranormal Romance -

Nathan's Heart / The Brotherhood of Bandits

About the Author

M. Malone is a RITA® Award winner and a NYT & USA Today Bestselling author of completely inappropriate romantic comedy. She spends most days wearing Wonder Woman leggings and T-shirts that she's embarrassed for anyone to see while she plays with her imaginary friends.

She lives with her husband and their two sons in the picturesque mountains of Northern Virginia even though she is afraid of insects, birds, butterflies and other humans.

She also holds a Master's degree in Business from a prestigious college that would no doubt be scandalized at how she's using her expensive education.

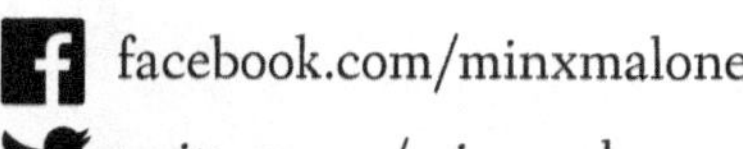 facebook.com/minxmalone

twitter.com/minxmalone

 instagram.com/minxmalone

bookbub.com/authors/m-malone